Chasing Roses

JUDY TURNER FRAIZER

Tate Publishing & *Enterprises*

Chasing Roses

This title is also available as a Tate Out Loud product. Visit www.tatepublishing.com for more information.

Published by Tate Publishing & Enterprises, LLC
127 E. Trade Center Terrace | Mustang, Oklahoma 73064 USA
1.888.361.9473 | www.tatepublishing.com

Tate Publishing is committed to excellence in the publishing industry. The company reflects the philosophy established by the founders, based on Psalms 68:11,

"The Lord gave the word and great was the company of those who published it."

Cover design by Jacob Crissup
Interior design by Janae J. Glass

Published in the United States of America

ISBN: 978-1-60462-149-5
1. Fiction: Action & Adventure 2. Fiction: Romance

07.09.04

Chasing Roses is dedicated to the very special kids in my life: Sebastian, Victoria, Madison, and Brooklyn Gordon, my great nephew and nieces; and to my grandchildren: Allison Fraizer, Jake and Jessica Simpson, Brandon Welborn, and Cole Welborn. I love each of you beyond words.

Also dedicated to the wonderful Kentucky Horse Park in Lexington, Kentucky, home to three of my most special friends: John Henry, DaHoss, and Cigar. Make plans to visit them soon. www.kentuckyhorsepark.com

And in loving memory of Barbaro, Pine Island, Three Degrees, SweetPie, and all of the other wonderful horses who have galloped through our lives and now peacefully graze in heaven's green pastures.

ACKNOWLEDGEMENTS

I want to thank my Lord and Savior Jesus Christ for my salvation; what peace to know I will spend eternity with Him!

I also want to thank my mother Gwenda Simpson for her love and support, emotional as well as financial.

And in random order, I want to recognize:

Irwin Colgin, one of my dearest friends and traveling companion. With him, his friendship, and his support for more than thirty-eight years, I have been able to do research for this novel. I look forward to many more years of the same.

Ron Gordon, my brother-in-law. He listened to the story idea and cncouraged me by telling everyone, "This is the one!" It gave me the courage to sit down and write it. And my sister Suzan, who is, and has always been, a source of love and support for all of us.

My brother Rusty Simpson and his wife Linda for taking care of the grandkids and Mom, and for doing God's work in Ghana.

My friend, co-worker, and fellow writer, Tim McCord, for working long hours editing, making suggestions, and offering encouragement. I look forward to doing the same for him on his new novel.

Gary and Angie Stevens, for reading the story and asking for more. I wrote this to be a movie for you to star in, Gary. Forever in my heart, *you* are Stone Hardaway.

The Grown-up "Kids:" Melissa, David, Robynn, and Myndi.

Stan, Gerry, Bernie, Norm, Donna Cheryl Wilkins, Player, Bright stripe, my friends at www.winninggonewild.com and to my good friend and agent, Pamela Thornbury for their friendship, ideas, and the fun we are going to have selling books and making movies!

My special new friend and editor, Amanda Webb. You are the *best*!

And to Brian and Michael Bergstrom, Steve Fisher and all my co-workers at SecureNet, Inc., and Open Options, Inc. who have encouraged me. You probably don't know what you mean to me. Now you do!

PREFACE

Dear Reader:

I wrote *Chasing Roses* originally to be a film opportunity for Gary Stevens, a retired jockey, who also co-starred in the movie *Seabiscuit.* I continue to hold on to the hope that Gary will get to play the role of Stone Hardaway.

My next novel is in progress. I hope to have it finished and into publication by mid-2008.

I have been writing since I was a child and while I have had poetry published; this is my first full-length novel.

I write each day in my professional career, what a blessing to get to do what you love.

I am living proof that our abilities are absolutely *God*-given. I hope I have brought the characters in this story to life for you.

Thank you for reading *Chasing Roses.*

—Judy

ONE

The children argued over a box of cereal but Sandy just stood at the kitchen window, staring out at nothing in the yard. When she heard the crash, she turned to see Stoney shuffling from one foot to the other, the small toy from the cereal box clutched in his hand, which he quickly hid behind his back, and Emma staring at her with wide-eyes. Both children were looking at her with fear on their faces. She tried not to smile at them. Those big blue eyes staring at her as if she might eat them alive. She loved Emma's blond curls, which curved around her little cheeks, and Stoney's strong jaw, such a handsome little man. He was going to be tall, and not so thin like Bobby. Sometimes she loved them so much she could hardly contain it in her heart. And sometimes, like today, when she was so tired her brain felt numb, she wished they just wouldn't fuss and argue.

"Who spilled the cereal?" she asked.

Stoney looked at his sister, then back to his mother, and said, "We both did, but it was mostly my fault."

Sandy walked over to the table with a dishrag and began to clean up the mess. She knew she should fuss at the kids but she was just too tired. "You two know you aren't supposed to take the toy out of the cereal without asking."

"I am sorry, Mommy," Emma said softly.

"Me too, Mom," Stoney said. "It really was an accident."

"I know, I know, but I have told you a hundred times not to fight at the table."

Stoney looked at Emma and said quietly, "I am sorry, Emma. You can have the prize this time."

Emma took the small toy from her brother's hand and whispered, "Thank you."

"Are you guys finished eating?"

The kids nodded and Stoney asked if they could go to the barn and play.

Sandy told them to be careful, and for Stoney to watch his sister. She watched them as they ran out the front door and she thought how lucky she was to have such great kids, even messy and fussy as they were sometime.

She wiped the table and threw the milk-soaked cereal in the trash, then retreated to the living room and lay down on the sofa.

Sandy rested her head on the sofa pillow and tried

to sleep, but dark shadows clouded her dreams. Everywhere she looked, she saw a scowling, leering face. And in the back of her mind, she could hear the dogs whining and barking. She just wished they would shut up.

The kids ran to the barn, eager to see Tom Cross, the ranch foreman, who was happy as always to see them. He had worked on this farm and taken care of their father as a boy. Now Mr. Tom, as the kids called him, was enjoying them as much as he did his own grandchildren.

He bustled around the barn, impressing them with some of his cowboy tricks, rope-tying, and lasso-making. But they soon tired of that, so he shooed them off to play in the hayloft then went back to work.

Stoney especially loved the hayloft. He told Emma he could see far, far away when he looked out the big window. And when he lay on the floor, he could see through the slats down into the barn below. The hay smelled good. He could lay there for hours watching the horses stand in their stalls and the chickens meander in and out. He also had fun spying on Mr. Tom. Occasionally, little pieces of hay would slip through the cracks. Stoney always tried to hide when Mr. Tom would look up and smile at him.

Emma was four and she followed him everywhere. He was almost six and he knew his little sister thought he was the smartest boy in the world. Rather than thinking she was a pain to have around, he took special care of her. His dad told him it was his job to watch out for her when he wasn't at home. Stoney took the job very seriously. The steps to the hayloft were old and rickety and Stoney knew that one bad step could send her falling to the stone floor below. So, he watched her like a hawk as they climbed the steps. He always let her go first so if she slipped, he could catch her.

Emma wasn't afraid of the old steps that took her to their hideout. The hayloft held her treasures: a mother cat and six tiny kittens.

It had rained the night before and there was a wonderful aroma in the barn. The hay smelled good; and the breeze that blew in the big open window brought the fragrance of the big pine trees and the beautiful flowers that grew on their farm.

Emma loved to smell the kittens; she would even kiss them until Stoney told her that it was gross. She still kissed them; she just didn't let him see her. Now as she leaned against a bale of hay, the kittens played in her lap with the mother cat laying a few feet away keeping a watchful eye on her babies.

Stoney was sitting against another bale looking at a magazine he had brought from the house. It was of motorcycles. He and his dad wanted a motorcycle but his mother said, *never!* So they just looked at the magazines, talked secretly about them, and dreamed.

It was very quiet, neither child talked; so they heard the truck pull onto the drive long before it reached the barn. Tom had his radio blaring country music so he didn't hear it. Stoney peeked out the barn window and saw a pick-up pulling into the barnyard with a trailer hitched to it. It wasn't Uncle Don's truck; it was just like his dad's, but his dad couldn't be home yet. *Maryland is a faraway state,* his mother had said. He figured it was one of the Dowd's farm hands. Maybe they were bringing more horses from their barn. It had been such a mess after the fire. Stoney remembered his mom and dad crying because Uncle Don's oldest horse had died from the smoke. He peeked again from his secret place in the loft and was surprised to see the guy they had met at the supermarket get out of the truck. He hadn't liked that man at all. He was crippled; he said he fell off a horse. And the man made his mother mad because he talked bad words in front of them and then he even made *her almost* say a bad word. Stoney just knew that guy had no business here.

Emma ran over to the hayloft window to see what was going on but Stoney stopped her. "Go hide in the hay, Emma, and don't come out till I tell you to." She looked at him for a moment as if thinking about arguing with him, but something in his voice told her to do as he said. So she ran and hid in her favorite hiding place behind the stacked bales of hay.

Stoney watched through the cracks in the loft floor as the guy wandered with his distinctive limp inside the barn. Tom hadn't seen him yet. Just as he turned around, the guy hit him over the head with a shovel. Stoney gasped and then raced over to the fireman's pole he used to slide down to the barn. Emma wasn't supposed to use it; Daddy said it was dangerous, but sometimes she did just because it was fun. And it was a fast way to get out when mom was calling them.

By the time Stoney landed on the floor, Matt Stanley had FlintRemembered and was already outside by the trailer.

Stoney ran up to him, "Why did you hit Mr. Tom? Why did you hit him, you mean old...and that's not your horse, you just put him right back in his stall!"

Without a thought Matt said, "I am just borrowing him, kid, your daddy said I could come get him."

"No he didn't, you put him back. He's not even my daddy's horse! He's my Uncle Don's horse!"

Matt loaded the horse into the trailer, slammed the trailer door closed, and said, "Get out of my way, you little brat."

Stoney stepped in front of him with his hands on his hips and glared at Matt, "You are stealing that horse, mister, and stealing is wrong!"

"I said for you to move kid." That made Stoney even more determined to stop him, and he tried to slam the open door of the truck so Matt couldn't get in. Matt grabbed him by the arms and threw him in the front seat of the pickup. Stoney tried kicking him, but Matt slapped him. Stoney's lip started to bleed.

Matt climbed in the truck and pushed Stoney against the seat. Stoney reached for the door handle on the passenger side to try to open it and jump out, but Matt grabbed him by the shirt and gave him a maniacal grin, "Looks like you are going with me." Matt turned the truck and trailer around in the big circle driveway, pulled out of the gate, and sped off down the highway.

"My mouth is bleeding," Stoney sobbed.

"You're lucky I didn't knock all of your teeth out. I told you to get out of the way and, besides, you tried to kick me first!"

Emma watched from the window in the barn as the truck raced off down Hopsend Road.

She grabbed the fireman's pole with shaky hands and held on as tight as she could until she reached the barn floor and ran over to Tom. "Tom, Mister Tom, get up!"

He was alive, but out cold.

Emma ran from the barnyard to the house yelling for her mom. "Mommy, Mommy, that man took Stoney, he took Stoney!"

Sandy was still on the sofa, half-asleep. When she heard Emma crying, she was terrified that Stoney had fallen and was hurt.

She sat up as Emma ran to her side, "That man took Stoney and FR. Stoney tried to stop him and he took him, too, and he hurt Mister Tom."

"What are you talking about Emma? What man?" Sandy couldn't breathe. "Who took Stoney?"

"That man that made you say the bad word in the store, he took him."

Sandy felt like she was going to faint. She raced to the phone and called the police. After she reported the kidnapping, she ran to the barn to check on Tom, dialing Bobby's cell phone number as she ran.

As soon as he heard her voice, Bobby was filled with fear. He wished he could close his eyes and ears and pretend he didn't have to listen, like a child wishing he could just make it go away. The guilt of not being able to get back home after the race in Maryland had kept him awake all night. He had paced the floor worrying about his family and hoping that everything would be fine when he did get home. He had been feeling an angst that he couldn't explain. He knew that part of it was being worried about leaving Sandy and the kids alone, while knowing Matt Stanley had come back to Kentucky yet not knowing where he was or what he was up to.

Sandy was hysterical. She bent over Tom, who had a very bad cut on his head. She heard the sirens in the distance. She handed Emma the phone and, as her little girl held the phone to her face, she propped Tom's head up with her arm and screamed to the phone, "He took Stoney. He took our little boy. Come home Bobby, please come home! What do I do Bobby? Help me. Help me, Bobby please!"

"What do you mean, 'took him'? Who took him Sandy, who took him?"

"Matt Stanley. He took Stoney and he stole Flint Remembered."

Bobby screamed into the phone, "I am going to kill him. I am coming home and I will hunt him down and kill him."

"*Come home, Bobby*!" Sandy screamed.

. . .

It was the middle of the afternoon before Bobby and Don Dowd could get home from Maryland.

Emma ran to Bobby as soon as he got out of the Dowd's car.

"Daddy, that man made mommy say a bad word and then he put Stoney in his truck and went away. And he took Uncle Don's horsey too."

"You saw him, Emma?"

"Uh huh, she nodded. Stoney made me stay in the hay with the kittens, but he went to make that man put the horsey back."

"Oh my, Lord, Bobby said, Emma I am proud of you for being a good girl and listening to your brother. Did you tell the policeman what color that bad man's truck was?"

"It was black, just like your truck, Daddy."

So this was how he got in the gate at the Dowd's and managed to make it to the barns—everyone thought it was me, Bobby realized.

Sandy ran to him and he held her close. "Hey," he said softly. "Are you okay?"

"Yes," she whispered. "I just can't believe this. It's just a nightmare that won't go away, Bobby."

"I know, baby, but we will find him. Where could he have gone?" Bobby asked.

"The police came right away and called in the FBI, but they said he still had a good head start." Sandy sobbed, "I hope our baby is all right, I just can't understand why Matt would do this."

"Because he's not right in his head, Sandy. We have known that for a long time. He's just crazy."

Sandy started to cry again, "Crazy doesn't help me,

Bobby. If he's so crazy, how do we know he won't do something to Stoney? Something terrible?"

Bobby didn't speak; he just pulled his wife close to him and let her cry it out. He wondered the same thing and it scared him to even think about it.

"I am so worried about Emma," Sandy sobbed. "She's only four years old, Bobby. She watched her brother being kidnapped. He might have taken her too if Stoney hadn't hid her. That's a lot for a baby to handle."

Emma stared up at her parents with wide eyes. She didn't like this. She didn't like not knowing where Stoney was and if that bad man would hurt him. She didn't like to see her mommy cry and she could see her daddy shaking like he was cold. It made her stomach hurt.

Bobby said, "Honey, the FBI are pros at this type of thing. They are going to find him—it's just a matter of time. We just have to wait now and that's the worst part. They are searching the country for him."

Bobby waited until Sandy quieted down before he asked her, "Where were the dogs, Sandy? I thought they would have surely scared him away. Danny would have eaten him up. I can't believe they let him get away."

Sandy said, "I know the FBI said they are searching the country for him but it still makes me afraid. And I feel guilty because I put the dogs in the back to keep them from barking at the cats in the hayloft. I know Danny would never have even let him out of his truck, but I kept him penned up."

Bobby nodded. "Don't blame yourself, you had no way of knowing the creep would come here, I am the one to blame for going to Maryland when you asked me not to leave you!"

He couldn't stop shaking; he was trying to be strong for his family, but he felt like he let them down by going away, even if the plan had been to just be gone for one day.

They went back to the living room. Bobby sat down at the dining room table with Agent Sharp from the FBI and one of his associates.

Special Agent Robert Sharp was a middle-aged man, all business and all Bureau. He had started with the FBI right out of college and was the Special Agent in charge of the eastern region of the United States. Everyone seemed to know and respect him. He had been very sweet to Emma and Sandy and tried to be as reassuring as he could with Bobby, but he believed in always playing his cards straight. He didn't downplay the danger he felt their little boy was facing.

Sharp looked over his shoulder and saw Sandy and Emma sitting on the couch with both dogs at their feet and said in a low voice to Bobby, "We have had a couple more reports of people seeing the truck and trailer, Bobby."

Bobby wondered why he would whisper if the news was good. "But?" Bobby asked, fearful of the answer.

"No reports of a child with the man from either witness."

Bobby's heart sank.

Agent Sharp reached over to pat Bobby's shoulder. "Hey, these are unconfirmed reports, remember.

We haven't gotten confirmation of the license plate or even anyone who can agree that the trailer was a horse trailer. People get all up in arms when we issue an Amber Alert. They want so badly to help find the kids that they sometimes see what their minds want them to see."

Bobby nodded. "What do you really think Agent Sharp? Please just tell me the truth."

Agent Sharp cleared his throat and glanced back over at Sandy and Emma. "The truth is, the longer it takes to track him down the worse the outcome can be. We know this guy hates you. He's tried to ruin you. He's had it in his mind to steal your life, your wife, and your kids. We just can't know what else he might do. What I can't understand is why he stole that horse. It's just going to slow him down. He can't possibly get very far without someone spotting him."

Bobby nodded. "I don't know how he knew the horse was here in my barn. He's not even my horse."

Agent Sharp said, "Can you tell me about the horse he stole when he was a kid? I am just trying to put this puzzle together in my mind."

"He stole my Grandfather's prize horse. It was the farm's top stallion," Bobby answered. That horse was a Kentucky Derby winner, like this one, and had a pedigree second to none. Every horseman in the country with a mare to breed wanted to use him. The stallion was my grandfather's bread and butter. Matt Stanley came to live with his uncle about the same time my mother and I came to live with my Grandfather, right after my father was killed in a motorcycle accident. My grandfather and Max Stanley were big buddies. They drank together and played cards nearly every day. Matt and I played together. He told me his mother was in an asylum. I was only twelve years old and had no idea what an asylum was. My mother was always real sweet to him and I think he really loved her, like she was the mom he didn't have. Max was a mean old codger. He had plenty of money, or so he made out, and he treated Matt like he was dirt. You could tell he didn't really want the kid around, so he was always pounding on him and yelling at him. My grandfather acted just the opposite to me. I was all he had left in the world after my dad died. I think it made Matt jealous that people loved me. I went to summer camp with a group from my church and was gone for two weeks. When I came back, I just heard bits and pieces about Matt and the horse, and the next time I saw him, which was months later, he walked with a limp from where he had fallen with the stallion.

"Old Max and Grandfather worked out some kind of arrangement to pay for the medical bills, but the stallion had to be put to sleep after Matt fell with him, and that's when my Grandfather started losing money. Things stayed pretty much the same until I was sixteen when Grandfather died and mother and I moved to Florida. I saw Max after the funeral, and Matt was with him, but he wouldn't speak to me. Mother sold this place to Max and we left."

Agent Sharp shook his head, "You never really did anything to him except befriend him?"

"I was just his friend. I can't figure it out, Agent Sharp."

"Sometimes there's nothing that can explain the behavior of a person with a sick mind, they just conjure up their own dragons. You happen to be Matt Stanley's dragon, Bobby."

Sandy walked over to the table and stood behind Bobby, "I am going to put Emma to bed. She is exhausted."

"Why don't you try to get some rest too, Mrs. Tolliver?" Agent Sharp asked her.

She stared at him for a moment and then she said, "No, I am okay. I want to hear every word."

Emma ran over to her daddy and he grabbed her and gave her a hug. "Sleep tight, my big girl," he said.

"Tomorrow I think Stoney will be home," she said softly.

"We hope so, honey. You say a prayer for him, okay?"

She nodded and Sandy took her hand and they went down the hall.

"She is one bright little girl," Agent Sharp said. "She gave us some information that I am not sure an adult could have remembered."

Bobby smiled, "Yes, they are both very bright."

Agent Sharp looked at Bobby, "Do you think Stoney is being...well...how shall I phrase this? Being quiet and not aggravating this character even more? I guess what I am wondering is if Stoney can keep his cool?

This will be a lot easier for him I think if he just keeps quiet. You know, not crying?"

Bobby said, "Stoney is a calm kid. I am sure he's scared out of his wits. I just have to trust that he's doing okay." And deep in his heart, he prayed that he was.

When Sandy came back from Emma's room, she sat down beside Bobby on the couch and rested her head in his lap. He stroked her hair as they both stared into the empty fireplace. In a few minutes, he could tell she had fallen asleep. She was so tired; Bobby didn't know how she was managing to keep herself together. He was all tied up in knots inside, feeling a rage he had never experienced before.

As he stroked her hair, he thought about Matt Stanley and how much he had come to despise him. He wondered what could have produced such hate. Sandy stirred in her sleep; Bobby leaned over and kissed her ear. She was so beautiful; he couldn't blame Matt for wanting his life. But it hadn't always been like this. He could remember when he left this farm wondering if he would ever see it again.

TWO

Somehow, Bobby managed to get through the funeral and was even able to smile and thank the people who spoke so highly of his grandfather.

After the funeral, while people were at the house to pay their last respects Bobby overheard two men talking about wanting to buy the farm. He couldn't believe that they would have the nerve to stand here in the living room of his grandfather's house and talk like that.

Bobby felt a responsibility to his mother, to the ranch hands, and to his grandfather's legacy to carry on as if things were still the same. Even though just a teenager, he had every intention of them staying right where they were and running things just as they had been doing for the past months.

Bobby stepped outside to talk to Tom. Tom could keep the foreman's job and maybe they could get more horses; they had to do something to generate a good income for them.

Tom loved Bobby like a son and he respected Grandfather Tolliver. He didn't let on to Bobby that he, and most of the other hands, had worked for several months without pay; unbeknownst to Bobby, his grandfather was deeply in debt. Ever since that Stanley kid had been hurt and they had lost the stallion, things had gone downhill, a little at a time.

After things settled down, and Joy and Bobby found out about the financial problems, his mother tried very hard to salvage the place by selling a few of the horses they had left. She tried to arrange to pay the debts off. But in the end, they had no choice but to sell to Max Stanley. Old Max did assure Bobby if he ever wanted to come back and buy the place that he would sell it to him, no questions asked.

His mother decided they would move to Florida and live with her sister Iris. This was the only home Bobby had really ever known and he loved it. The thought of leaving was almost more than he could stand. But he had no choice; so with a broken heart, Bobby left Kentucky and moved to Miami, Florida.

Bobby wanted to hate Florida. He knew it was childish, but he needed an outlet for his pain and anger. Florida was going to be it. He made up his mind to dislike it and be as miserable as he could the entire time he was there. *That,* he thought, *will serve everyone right for taking me so far away from home.* He was tight-lipped on the trip and spoke to his mother only when she spoke to him. It made him even angrier that she seemed almost giddy to be leaving Kentucky. She was talkative and happy. She sang old songs along with the radio and tried to pull Bobby out of his depression. He wanted to be miserable for a while. Her happiness only served to make him unhappier.

He finally asked her if she wasn't sad about Grandfather dying. She told him that, of course, she was sad about Grandfather, he had been very good to them. Then he asked her if she wasn't sad about leaving the farm. Joy thought for a few minutes and then told Bobby that she hated to leave the farm because of him; but for herself, she was glad to be gone. She told him that she hoped he would forgive her for not loving the place as he had. It took Bobby a little while to realize the difference between how he had felt about it and how she had felt about it. It was never her home, but it was the only home he had ever known.

He hoped that one day his mother would forgive him for being so angry about the move. But his guilt wasn't going to diminish the pain of separation. They drove a number of miles in silence again, and then Bobby got his first glimpse of the Atlantic Ocean. He hadn't been prepared for it. It was an amazing sight. He took in everything. The golden sand, the deep blue water, the sand dunes, and waving palm trees. Suddenly, a sense of peace overtook him. He was just amazed at the vastness of it. He told his mother that it seemed to go on forever, and just fall over the edge of the earth.

Joy smiled as she watched him take it all in with an open mouth. It was overwhelming. They had been taking turns driving but now he just sat and stared out the passenger window past his mother, like a little boy seeing something magical. How could something like seeing the ocean for the first time have such a profound effect on him? He didn't know why, but he relaxed and let the peace cover his senses like a soft blanket.

Aunt Iris's neighborhood was very nice. She lived in a gated community with an armed guard. The homes were expensive and luxurious, and her house was just across the street from the beach. As they pulled into her drive, Bobby admired the landscaping and the colorful flowers.

"It isn't what you expected, is it?" his mother asked. Bobby had to admit that he was more than a little surprised. Iris seemed genuinely happy to have them come to Florida. Bobby had not seen his aunt in several years. Not since after her husband died and she had visited Kentucky to get away from everything for a while. Joy told Bobby that Iris had been very lonely and Bobby wondered why she had stayed in this huge house all alone. Maybe it was just full of memories, like home in Kentucky. Aunt Iris greeted them both with hugs. She showed them around the house and got Bobby settled in his room. She told him to feel free to raid the fridge anytime he felt like it.

Bobby knew he would take her up on that offer. His bedroom was large and spacious with windows all along the eastern wall. He had his own bathroom, a huge closet, a desk, a telephone, and a TV. He wasn't used to such luxury and, for a few minutes, thought that he might just like it here. The farm had always been nice, but after grandfather lost his wife and then the stallion, he hadn't seemed to care about such things; the house Bobby grew up in was not as elegant as it had been when grandmother was alive. But Iris's home was really lovely.

The housekeeper made a special meal for them to share later. In the meantime, he helped his mother unpack the car, arranged his room, and put away his things. He didn't think he was going to be here long; soon he would graduate and he had already decided he would be going back to Kentucky. But he would make the best of it while he was here. His intention of making everyone around him miserable since he was so miserable now seemed a distant memory.

As he stared out the window of his room, Bobby felt a strong desire to go walk in the sand and wade in the ocean. But he was very tired. It had been a long trip and he felt emotionally drained. He decided to eat a bite of dinner, then go to bed. The ocean would certainly be there tomorrow.

When the sun came up, Bobby woke and immediately went to the window. It was a glorious day in Florida and he couldn't wait to get out and look around. He was ready for his walk on the beach. He dressed quickly and left the house.

A few people were already on the beach, all dressed in swimsuits, or shorts and sandals. Bobby felt a few strange looks. He found it was not only difficult to walk in the sand in his cowboy boots, but also that he looked ridiculous, so he sat down and took them off. He rolled up the legs of his jeans and started walking along the edge of the water, trying to ignore the stares. Every few feet he ventured just a little farther out into the water and then ran back in with the waves. He felt like a little kid with the water splashing on his legs, soaking the cuffs of his jeans. He forgot for a few minutes that he was supposed to be unhappy and instead delighted himself in the wide expanse of blue-green ocean and the feel of the feather-soft sand beneath his feet. He got wet from head to toe from the waves crashing around him as he ventured farther and farther out into the water. He took off his wet shirt and threw it on the beach. He didn't even realize no one else was in the water. Everyone just watched him play like a little kid. He felt a serenity that had eluded him for a long time.

"Hey, be careful!" someone yelled. "Didn't you see the sign?"

Bobby turned around to see a pretty teenage girl standing a few feet behind him. She was very tiny and petite, almost like a child; but he realized she was about the same age as he was. She had the sweetest face and big blue eyes. Her blond hair was pulled back in a ponytail and she looked like she had just been out of bed for a few minutes. Bobby thought she was the prettiest girl he had ever seen.

"What did you say?"

She smiled at him. "There are jelly fish in the water,

millions of them. That's why there are signs to warn people not to get in the water along here."

Bobby jumped out of the water "Jelly fish? What do they do to you?"

The girl laughed. "Why, they sting your little toesies."

"Thanks for getting me out of there. I must look pretty stupid, huh?"

"Not stupid. Just a lot like a tourist."

"Hmmm, well, that's where you are wrong. I live here," Bobby said with a snort. Then he grinned. "Well, for a day I've lived here. I just moved in with my Aunt." He pointed to Iris' house.

"Oh, I'll bet that you are Bobby from Kentucky, aren't you?" Bobby was surprised that she knew his name but he nodded. She stuck out her hand. "I'm Sandy Wagner. My dad and I live two doors down from Iris. She and my dad are old friends," she continued. "We've heard about you and your mom for a long time. In fact, we are having you all over for a BBQ at our house tomorrow night."

Bobby wasn't sorry to hear that, he had to admit to himself. He and Sandy stood a few feet from the edge of the water, just out of reach of the jellyfish, and talked a while longer and then she told him she had to go. He said to her before she could leave, "When will I be able to go in the water?"

She said with a smile, "I will take you to a beach where everyone hangs out in a day or two, if you want. If you don't surf, you can use a boogie board. It's a lot of fun."

"Sounds great," Bobby said. He didn't tell her that

he didn't surf, didn't know what a boogie board was, and didn't even own a swimsuit. *I think I better find a store and do some shopping.*

As Sandy walked away, she thought to herself, *Oh boy, I am in big trouble.* She laughed at that thought and ran the rest of the way to her house.

Craig Wagner noticed her flushed face when she entered the kitchen. "Hey," he said. "What happened to you?"

"Nothing," she lied. "I just ran over from the beach. Just a bit out of breath."

Craig stared at her a minute. "Looks like you might have met a boy on the beach."

"*Dad*! Were you spying on me?"

He laughed. "No, I just walked out front to get the paper. Who is the boy?"

"It's Iris' nephew Bobby."

"Why are you so red? Is he *real* cute?" He teased her.

"*Dad!*" she said with a laugh. Then she smiled a dreamy smile. "But yes, he is *very* cute."

Craig frowned at the look on Sandy's face. *Well this looks like it might be trouble.* But it made him happy to hear Sandy laughing.

When Bobby got back to the house, he told Aunt Iris about meeting Sandy. Iris told him all about Sandy and her family. Iris had a great deal of respect for Craig Wagner, a very successful investment broker who had raised Sandy all alone. They were a very nice family.

Iris was amused when she saw the twinkle in his eye as he talked about her. And she thought to herself,

I'd bet that pretty little girl can help heal the hurting heart of this Kentucky boy.

The next morning, Aunt Iris took Bobby to the nearest shopping mall and helped him select some things more appropriate for sunny Florida. Like a boogie board. And a swimsuit.

Bobby enjoyed the ride with Aunt Iris. Her community was such a nice area with the houses and stores to his right and the ocean to his left. Hard to pay attention when you can't take your eyes off the view. There were a lot of pretty girls in shorts and bikini tops to catch his eye too, but something about that pretty Sandy made the others seem almost unappealing. Bobby thought about her promise to take him to the beach and it made him happy. Maybe the move to Florida wouldn't be so bad after all. At least for a while.

When they got back home, Bobby went upstairs to put away his things. When he came down, his mother and Aunt Iris were giggling. It was nice to hear his mother laugh. It had been a long time since he had seen her look as content as she did now. She seemed to look younger in just the short time they had been here. Maybe the farm and all the burdens on her had been too much. At least she could stay here with Iris as long as she wanted. And maybe she would not feel as if the weight of the world was on her shoulders. Bobby felt bad for feeling so sorry for himself earlier on the drive from Kentucky, but she didn't seem to remember.

Aunt Iris told him about the BBQ at Sandy's house and he told her that he already knew about it. Joy was very nervous about going. She had the distinct impression that Iris had something up her sleeve, perhaps trying to play cupid with Craig Wagner and her.

Bobby hoped she would play cupid with him and Sandy, but he wasn't sure they would need cupid at all.

When they got to the Wagner's for the BBQ, Sandy introduced Bobby to her father. Bobby liked him immediately, and so did his mother. He noticed that they were an instant couple, with Craig spending all his time with her. Even while he cooked, Joy stood at his side, listening intently as he talked. *Well,* Bobby thought to himself, *this might be something special.*

He hoped his mother would find someone. He had never understood why she didn't go out on dates. She had seemed quite content to take care of him and grandfather. And as children often fail to do, he didn't really think of Joy as a person with feelings and emotions and her own life to live; she was just "mom." Now as he watched her talking to Craig, he saw a very attractive woman and felt bad that she had missed so much.

Iris watched Craig and Joy too. She had hoped that these two would hit it off. They both needed someone, and she thought they were perfect for each other. Playing cupid a little bit didn't hurt anything. And there was Sandy and Bobby. Even from across the room, Iris could see Bobby's eyes shining as he talked to Sandy. It wasn't long before Iris looked up and saw they were gone. When she looked for them, she saw them walking along the beach, holding hands.

It was love at first sight for Bobby and Sandy. Two

like souls found each other. If anything, they should be envied, not just for finding love but for having their entire lives ahead of them to spend with each other. Sandy and Bobby talked as they sat side by side at a picnic table. Neither seemed to care that there was a barbeque going on and their families were expecting them to participate; they had finally found each other and had seventeen years to catch up on.

Even Craig who was so protective of his daughter, even more than some men tend to be, had to admit that Bobby seemed like a great kid. Craig relaxed. Maybe he was too busy thinking about the lovely Joy Tolliver to be very concerned about a couple of teenage kids. Even if one of them was his daughter, who was alone on a beach with a teenage boy.

After the BBQ, as Sandy and Craig cleaned up, she told her dad all about Bobby. And when she mentioned that his greatest desire in life was to be a jockey and someday move back to Kentucky, Craig thought for a minute then said, "I should take him over to Calder and introduce him to Don Dowd."

"Oh daddy," Sandy bubbled, "that would be great!" As she raced toward the phone she asked, "What's a Calder and who is Don Dowd?"

Craig laughed and said, "Calder is a racetrack and Don is a horse trainer. He is a client of mine."

"Oh that's great! Can you take him tomorrow?"

"Whoa kiddo, I have to check my schedule, but I think I might can arrange that." Sandy grabbed the phone and called Bobby.

Bobby was thrilled. Not just that he was going to Calder, but that she had talked to Craig about him. She had really listened to his dreams. He thanked Sandy a dozen times before they hung up. He had hoped she would ride out to Calder with them, but she said she had already made plans with a girlfriend to go shopping. She told him that she would take him sightseeing in the afternoon when they got back. What she didn't say was that she wanted something new to wear to take him sightseeing. Suddenly everything in her closet seemed old and unattractive.

Bobby began to think and dream about Calder and meeting the trainer. He thought to himself that if the guy had any openings, he might just ask about a part-time summer job. As he crawled into bed, he realized that he had only been in Florida for a few days and was already happier than he ever thought that he could be. Isn't it just amazing what a beautiful girl can do for a young man's heart?

. . .

The eastern sky was bright as gold when he woke. He could smell the ocean and hear the waves crashing on the shore. This was going to be a great day. He and Craig were going to Calder this morning, then in the afternoon he and Sandy were going for a drive down the coast. He was dressed and waiting when Craig pulled his Lexus up to the front door. He leaned over, opened the passenger door, and told Bobby to get in.

They chatted like old friends on the fifteen-minute

ride to Calder. Craig seemed to know his way around the track. He pulled in the back near the barns and drove up toward the track.

"I called Don and told him we were coming," he said. "You'll like this guy. His family has been in the business a long time."

"What's his last name?" Bobby asked.

"Dowd," Craig said. "Don Dowd."

The name seemed to register in the back of Bobby's mind, but at that moment he saw the racetrack and a few horses galloping around and all else was forgotten. As Craig and Bobby walked toward the barns, a man walked toward them. He smiled and waved.

"That's Don," Craig said. When Don reached them, he shook hands with Craig, and then with Bobby as Craig introduced them. As they talked, Don mentioned that Bobby was from Kentucky. Bobby nodded. He told him where he was from and that he had grown up on his grandfather's farm. When Don asked him his grandfather's name, Don couldn't believe the coincidence.

"My dad used to buy horses from him," Don said. "I tagged along a few times. I remember your grandfather very well. I was very sorry to hear that he had passed away. My farm is not very far from there," Don said. "Most of the time my wife travels with me, but she decided to stay at home while we have these Florida meets going on; we have a mare about to foal and she wanted to be there with her. She is a real mother hen to our horses. Since the Calder season lasts so long,

I make frequent trips home or else she might forget what I look like."

Bobby thanked him for remembering his grandfather and then said, "I was hoping to find a job here at the track till I get out of school. I want to be a jockey."

"I can always use a good hand and, if you don't mind starting at the bottom, I will be happy to have you come on board. You are a good size to be a jockey. Tall, but not too tall, and thin as a rail."

Craig laughed, "I would love to be that thin. But I don't see that happening," and he patted his not-so-small belly.

"Good, clean living, Craig?" Don teased.

"Yeah, and good food, *lots* of good food." They all laughed. Craig's cell phone rang. He excused himself from Don and Bobby and walked away.

Don said, "Bobby, you look around all you want and then come see me in my office. I have some owners waiting for me, so I had better get back." He smiled, they shook hands again, and he walked away.

Bobby walked around for a few minutes, then went to the fence and watched the horses as they worked on the track. People were beginning to file in for the day's races and a couple of old men went to the fence a little farther down from Bobby. He could hear them talking about one horse in particular that was headed for a stakes race the following Saturday.

Another man stood at the rail, leaning against the fence. Bobby smiled and spoke to him. "They sure are beautiful when they run aren't they?"

The man stared at Bobby for a moment and then said, "I think they are beautiful all the time." He slowly smiled then said, almost as an afterthought, "But yes, they are especially beautiful when they run. It's what they were born to do."

Bobby agreed. "I have seen newborns struggle to stand up, as then as soon as they are a little steady on their feet, they want to run."

The man nodded. "They are real works of art."

Bobby looked at him and took a guess. "Are you a jockey, sir?"

The man offered a half smile. "I was a long time ago, but I have been out of racing for quite a while."

Bobby said, "I want to be a jockey. I want to be the best jockey in the world."

The man laughed. "Well that's a lofty ambition, kid. Good luck. It's a very hard business."

"This trainer we came out here to see is going to give me a job, so maybe in time I can make it," Bobby said. He noticed Craig put his cell phone away as he started walking back toward Bobby. "What's your name, sir?" Bobby asked.

"Stone," the man replied. "Stone Hardaway."

"It was nice meeting you, Mr. Hardaway." Bobby said as he turned to meet Craig and tell him that Don had said to meet him at his office in the barns. He turned to say goodbye to Stone, but the man had already walked away.

"I met a man who used to be a jockey."

Craig looked at the fence. As they walked off he said,

"Oh yeah? Those old guys just can't let go. I often see retired jockeys at the track. It's like what they live for."

Don Dowd told Bobby that he would have a job as long as Don's stock was in Florida. He asked Bobby to come to work the following day. Bobby rode home in Craig's Lexus, but his heart was floating on a cloud over Florida.

When Bobby got home, he couldn't wait to tell his mother and Aunt Iris about the job with Don Dowd. But he especially wanted to tell Sandy; it was her help, and her dad, that got him to Calder in the first place.

Joy Tolliver did not share Bobby's excitement about the part-time job with Don Dowd and the horses. She had hoped that this move would get the dream of becoming a jockey out of his mind. After he left the room, Iris scolded her.

"Joy Helen Tolliver! Shame on you! You had your dreams but you didn't live them, did you? Wasted your life on that spoiled rich kid from Kentucky, and then wound up a widow with nothing!"

"Iris!" Joy said, "I can't believe you'd say that!"

"Well it's true. I am sorry to be so blunt. But heck, why sugarcoat the truth?"

"That dream about law school was not my dream," Joy said. "It was mother and daddy's dream. I wanted to do nothing more than get married and be a housewife and mother. I had no desire to be a career-woman."

"Well, you got your wish," Iris said.

"Iris, weren't you ready for a normal home life after living with our parents?" Joy asked. "You must have been. That's what you did. You married Thomas and stayed home and kept house."

Iris looked at her and lit a cigarette. "Thomas and I wanted kids, we really did, and if we would have had kids then I would have been happy to stay at home, but Thomas couldn't make any babies. He always felt like he had cheated me, which was why he pampered me like he did. I would have enjoyed having a career, doing something worthwhile like being a nurse or something, but he wanted me right here." She took a deep drag of her cigarette and continued, "Mother and Daddy were always disappointed in me. Didn't matter that Thomas was successful and we had a lot of money. What mattered was that I didn't live up to their expectations."

Joy nodded. "I think they felt the same way about me."

Iris rolled her eyes. "Are you kidding? You were their hope, their fair-haired kid. All the dreams they had for both of us rested on your shoulders. You lived your dream then, if it was indeed your dream to be a wife and mother."

"It was, and while Bob was alive, I was happy," Joy replied.

Iris wasn't so sure her sister was telling the truth about that, but she didn't say anything else about it. It's one thing to know the truth and say it; it's quite another to let someone believe their own lies. There would be no more words about it; Iris knew the truth. And so did Joy.

"Then let Bobby live his dream," Iris said. "And

remember: dreams change. He may fall in love here in Florida and never want to leave." And she smiled.

Joy laughed, "Yes, I saw the way they walked out of the party and off to the beach last night. For once, big sister, you may be right."

Iris picked a decorative pillow off the couch and threw it at her sister. "For once?"

And they both laughed. Joy and Aunt Iris were still acting very silly when Sandy pulled in the driveway and honked. Bobby ran out of the house with a wave and a call over his shoulder, "Don't wait up!"

Joy and Iris ran to the window and watched as Bobby climbed in beside Sandy. They did high-fives as the kids drove away.

THREE

Bobby started his job with Don Dowd the next morning and was only mildly surprised to see Stone Hardaway standing at the fence, just as he had the previous day. Bobby walked over to greet him. "Good morning, Mr. Hardaway."

Stone Hardaway smiled. "You know, you asked me my name yesterday but I don't know yours."

"I'm Bobby Tolliver."

"Good morning, Bobby Tolliver. I take it your interview with the trainer went well yesterday."

Bobby nodded. "I start my job with Don Dowd this morning. I'm gonna be an assistant groom. I am hoping that, after I prove myself, he will let me gallop some horses and do some other things." He grinned as he said, "Like let me be a jockey."

"Congratulations," Stone said. "The Dowd's are good people."

Bobby looked up and saw one of the other employees walking toward them, "Well, I better get out of here, don't want to get fired my first day."

"Take care, kid. I'll see you around."

Bobby waved at Stone as he walked away. Iggy, the groom who came to get him, turned and looked at where he was waving.

"Nice guy," Bobby said.

Iggy gave him a strange smile and nodded.

The first day was hard; Bobby had to get used to doing things that he had never been required to do on his farm. He had never mucked a stall nor bathed a horse in his life. It was hard work; when he got home that evening, he was exhausted.

Joy secretly hoped it wasn't what he expected and that he wouldn't want to go back.

But Bobby slept soundly and was up before sunrise the next morning, trying to navigate the unfamiliar streets of Miami to get back to work at Calder. He parked his mother's car and walked past some barns to the stable area assigned to Don Dowd.

He heard laughing and talking. The scents around him aroused his senses. Hay, horses, freshly brewed coffee. It brought back memories of the farm and of the men who had worked there. There was such camaraderie amongst the men who worked together. Bobby realized at that moment that he had missed the working kinship almost as much as he had missed the rolling hills and breathtaking beauty of Kentucky.

When you are seventeen years old, there are things that get past you. This was not one of those things. Bobby enjoyed the memories this moment helped him recall. As he turned the corner to go to the Dowd barns, he walked right into Stone.

"Whoa, sorry kid," Stone said.

"My fault, sir. I wasn't paying attention."

"How about we do away with the sir stuff and you just call me Stone? You make me feel so old!" Stone rolled his eyes and laughed.

"You got it, Stone," Bobby replied. "Do you work around here too?"

"Nah, I just come out, hang around, and get in everybody's way."

"How come you don't ride anymore?" Bobby asked, and then added, "If you don't mind me asking."

"I am way out of my prime, kid. I'll leave the riding to you young guys." They walked along toward Dowd's barns.

"Well, here we are," Bobby said. "Wanna come in and have a cup of coffee?"

"No, thanks, I better be on my way. Take care of yourself and remember that you are working with some very high-strung animals. With these horses, you have to really be on your toes or *they* will be on your toes!"

"I'll watch it," Bobby said. "You gonna be around later?"

"Sure, maybe I'll stop by and see how you're getting along." Stone reached over and patted Bobby on his arm, then walked away.

Bobby watched him for a minute and then went to work.

. . .

Life soon fell into a regular routine for Bobby. The months passed by so quickly Bobby couldn't believe they had been in Florida almost a year. He went to school, worked every weekend, dated Sandy every night that he could. He had only a semester left and then would be finished with high school. He couldn't wait. He and Sandy talked many long hours about what they would do when they graduated.

One evening as he talked about his dream, and he told her about Kentucky and the farm for the hundredth time, Sandy asked him about his college plans.

"I have no desire to go to college," he said. "I just want to be a jockey. And," he added sheepishly. "I want to marry you."

Sandy smiled as she leaned over to kiss him. "Well, you had better marry me, mister, or I will come hunt you down. Wherever you are," she added sadly.

"Don says I am doing really well," Bobby said. "I have been galloping horses for a while now, but don't tell my mom. She gets all freaked out every time I mention riding horses. I have been getting a lot of help from this guy I met out at the track. He used to be a jockey."

"Isn't that pretty dangerous?" Sandy asked him.

"What me galloping the horses or him being a jockey?" Bobby laughed.

"Both," Sandy said.

"Oh, it could be I guess," Bobby answered. "But Stone is teaching me how to make them relax. These horses get really anxious, they are very high-strung, and some of them they think they are supposed to take off and run as fast as they can as soon as they set foot on the track. It's hard to settle them down, but Stone just has this way with them that is almost like magic."

"Well, I am glad you have someone helping you who knows what they are doing," Sandy replied.

"I can't get Stone to talk much about himself, but I can tell from the way he talks about racing and the way he is around the horses that he must have been a great jockey."

"That name sure is familiar," Sandy said.

"I never heard of him, he said he was out of racing before I was born," Bobby said.

"Oh, well something about that name sure rings a bell, but I can't put my finger on it. It drives me crazy not to be able to remember something!"

"I will introduce you next time you are out there. Strange thing though. I wonder if there are hard feelings between him and Don, they never even speak to each other. Don just walks right by us and never even blinks an eye, like he is just ignoring him."

"What would they be at odds about?" Sandy asked.

"Who knows, this is a funny business. Not only is it very competitive but it takes a long time for these guys to trust you. The other guys have really been giving me fits. I guess it's because I am the rookie, but they sure like playing practical jokes on me."

Bobby walked Sandy to her door and kissed her goodnight.

"So, it's official then?" he asked.

"What's official?"

"You are gonna marry me one day?"

Sandy laughed. "Yeah, and I hope you don't make me wait till I am an old lady."

"I don't think that's going to happen," Bobby replied. "I would marry you tonight if I could."

"Whew," she said with a laugh. "Our parents would string us up!"

"Yes, I guess they would if they even noticed we were gone. What's up with them anyway?" Bobby asked. "They remind me of us, all smiles and sweet looks when they think no one is looking. Why don't they just admit they are crazy about each other and get on with it? They have dated almost every single night since we moved here."

"Oh, gosh Bobby, I love your mom! She is wonderful—but if they get married, we become sister and brother...that's pretty weird!"

Bobby laughed, "We would be step-sister and brother! At our age, no one would even think a thing about it. And besides, I saw you first!" He kissed her and said, "Quit worrying. If they say they are getting married, we will just run off and get married first. Deal?"

"Ok, Bobby Tolliver, you have a deal."

It wasn't long before Joy and Craig finally admitted that they couldn't live without each other and they set a wedding date for late summer. So, Bobby and Sandy set their date for late spring, but they didn't tell anyone. And Bobby told Sandy that no matter where he was, he would come for her, and they would be married.

It didn't exactly work out that way.

. . .

When Bobby went to work on Saturday morning, the first thing he did was look for Stone. He found him sitting on an empty row of seats in the grandstand, staring out at the track as a few horses worked.

He sat down and said, "Stone, I am thinking about getting married."

Stone laughed and said, "It's just hormones kid. You are pretty young to be thinking of getting married. Believe me, its hormones." Bobby wasn't sure whether he was kidding with him, or whether he was serious.

"I love my girl, Stone. I want to go back to Kentucky after I graduate, get my jockey license, and work the Kentucky tracks. But I want Sandy to go with me."

"I see," Stone said. "What does your mother think about this?"

"She has her own romance going with Sandy's dad."

Stone frowned and said, "How's that?"

"See, we met Sandy and her dad Craig when we first moved here. Sandy and I have been dating ever since. Now her dad, who has been divorced for years, and my mother, a widow, have fallen in love and are getting married in late summer."

"Sounds like a soap opera," Stone laughed.

Bobby laughed too. "I guess it does, but I am very serious. I knew the minute I saw Sandy that I didn't care if I ever dated another girl in my life. Stone, you ever been married?"

Stone shook his head and said, "I was going to get married, but something happened. Sometimes things don't always work out the way you plan them, kid. I don't know about your age and all, but I do know life is very short and if you and your girl—"

"Sandy" Bobby interjected.

"—Sandy," Stone continued. "If you know for certain that she's the one for you and you are the one for her, well shoot—I say go for it."

Bobby smiled, "Thanks, Stone."

"I don't know why you need my blessing," Stone said. "But you got it."

Bobby said, "You know, I never had a hero before, except maybe my Grandfather when I was a little kid, but you're everything I want to be."

Stone laughed, "How's that?"

"Good at what you do. I see you with the horses. You love them and it seems like they know it. You know so much about riding—how to bring out the best in each horse. I sure would have loved to see you ride."

Stone said, "Seems like a whole lifetime ago now, Bobby. But you know, I think your being here is good for me too. I get to teach someone who loves it as much as I do, and that brings me a great deal of pleasure. So, I guess that makes you my hero."

Bobby laughed. "I hope you're gonna be around a long time to help me."

"I'm not going anywhere for a while, kid, I will be around as long as you need me." Bobby thanked Stone and then went to work. Stone watched Bobby walk toward the barns and he smiled. The kid reminded him of him when he was just starting out: gung-ho and full of dreams. Stone thought about Angie. Bobby said something about Craig and Sandy that made him realize who he was talking about. Craig was Angie's brother.

He hadn't cared for the guy when he first met him, he reminded him of a snaky oil salesman.

But after he got to know Craig, he liked him. He did not care for his wife Suzanne at all and no amount of time was going to change his opinion of her. She was selfish, self-centered witch and he hated the way she treated Craig and Angie. He rarely had anything to say to her and sometimes it made Angie feel bad. But he told her it was better than saying what he felt like saying, and knowing Stone, she let it go at that. He was glad she wasn't around anymore. He couldn't see Suzanne making anything but trouble for Bobby and Sandy. Stone shook his head at what seemed to be an amazing coincidence.

Don Dowd called Bobby in to his office and told him that he was going to return to Kentucky after the Gulfstream meet in mid-April. He had a colt that he had nominated to The Kentucky Derby and he wanted to start working with him as soon as he got out of the training center. He told Bobby they would be moving most of the horses to Gulfstream in the next couple of weeks and he had a list of things for Bobby to do before they moved.

Bobby told him he would get right on it, but that he was going to ask Stone to help him when it came time to work the horses at Gulfstream. He added that since Stone had ridden there he would be a big help. Don was busy working and wasn't paying any attention to what Bobby was saying when he mumbled, "Sure, okay, that would be great."

"I don't know why you don't offer Stone a job, Mr. Don. He is here everyday, so he might as well be on the payroll. And he knows more than anybody I ever met about how to work these horses." Bobby added, "Well, for someone who isn't a trainer, I mean."

Don Dowd looked up from his mountain of paperwork. "Huh? What did you say?"

"Stone Hardaway, I said he ought to get a job here too, he knows so much about horses."

Don stared at Bobby for a minute. "What are you talking about Bobby?"

"Oh, nothing sir, I can see you are busy. I was just wishing Stone could go with us to Gulfstream and to Kentucky too, if I get to go."

Don scratched his head. "Did you say Stone Hardaway? You wish Stone Hardaway could go with us?"

"Yes sir," Bobby replied. "He has been teaching me

so much. I just hate to leave without him. He's just a heck of a nice guy."

Don Dowd sat for a full minute and stared at Bobby. "Come here a second," he finally managed. Bobby walked over to the corner alcove where Don' desk sat and he looked at him. Don took a big scrapbook out of the bottom desk drawer. "Here, take a look at some of these pictures."

Bobby was a little surprised, but sat down with the book and opened it. When he got to the third page he said with obvious delight, "Oh wow, there are a ton of pictures of Stone in here! I didn't know you trained horses he rode."

"My dad was the trainer Stone rode for," Don said.

"Does he still train?' Bobby asked.

"Ummm, no, he's retired. Where have you...uh... *seen* Stone, Bobby?"

"Why right here, he helps me everyday. You've walked right by him, but I always thought you had something on your mind. You never seemed to pay much attention to us." This conversation made Bobby wonder again if there wasn't something between the two men.

Don Dowd looked into Bobby's eyes. "So you are saying that this man right here," and he pointed to a picture in the scrapbook. "This man sitting on the horse in this picture is Stone Hardaway?"

Bobby scowled, "Yes sir, but why are you asking me all these strange questions?" Bobby suddenly wondered if a conman had taken him in, pretending to be a jockey. *But that couldn't be, Stone knew too much about horses. He had to be a real jockey. He had seen the pictures for crying out loud!*

"Well, Bobby," Don began and then his cell phone rang. "Excuse me a second." Bobby walked over to the door and opened it. Stone was standing near a stall rubbing the nose of a horse. He looked up when Bobby whistled. Bobby looked back at Don who was still talking and he walked over to the stall where Stone was standing.

"Stone, do you and Don Dowd have a feud of some kind going on?"

Stone squinted and said, "No. No, we sure don't. Why do you ask?"

"Well," Bobby said, "he acted very strange just now when I told him I wished he would give you a job. He even had me look at a scrapbook with pictures of you and point to the one that I thought was you. Is that weird or what?" Stone whistled under his breath. "Okay, what is it?" Bobby asked him. You steal his woman or something?" And he laughed.

Stone didn't smile, he just said, "No, kid, wasn't anything like that."

Don Dowd came to the door of his office and Bobby said, "Sorry Mr. D, I'll be right there." Bobby walked back to the office and Stone followed a few feet behind.

"Ok, now where were we?" Don asked.

"Well, I was asking about putting Stone to work and you were about to yell at me." Stone stood just inside the door.

"I wasn't going to yell at you, Bobby. I am just not sure what's going on."

Bobby was confused. "What don't you understand? Is it against the rules or something for him to be helping me? Like an insurance deal because he isn't on the payroll?" Stone laughed a quiet laugh and Bobby looked at him. "What is it?" Stone shrugged and said nothing but walked over behind Don Dowd and began to look at the scrapbook lying open on the corner of the desk.

Don said, "Okay, let me get this straight. Now just bear with me, okay?"

"Sure," Bobby said, still not quite sure if he was in trouble or whether Don Dowd was just being a jerk.

"You think you can see *and* talk to Stone Hardaway, is that right?"

Bobby thought he was kidding. "Well yeah, I do, what are *you* saying? You *can't* see him?" And he laughed. Don could tell by the expression on Bobby's face that he was being very sincere.

"Bobby, Stone Hardaway is dead."

Stone said, "Well shoot, you could have been a little more diplomatic than that."

Bobby looked at Don and then at Stone. "What are you talking about?"

"Sit down, Bobby," Don said and pointed to the chair. "Will you tell me the whole story? Just tell me why you think you can see Stone Hardaway."

Bobby sat down and then jumped right back up and said angrily, "Stone is standing right there, right beside your desk looking at that scrapbook. Now you are going to tell me that *you* can't see him? That he is dead?"

Don Dowd looked where Bobby pointed and said,

"Son, Stone Hardaway died in, hmmmm, 1975, yep, that's right, he died before the Kentucky Derby in 1975. He had a heart attack riding in a race in New York."

Stone looked at Bobby and said, "It wasn't a heart attack. It was an aneurysm."

Bobby said, "An aneurysm? What is an aneurysm?"

"Yes, that's right," Don said, snapping his fingers. "It sure was an aneurysm. That's when a vein bursts in your head, or heart, I can't remember what the doctor said exactly. But it sure happened quickly. He was riding KingFlint," he pointed to the horse in the picture Bobby had identified. "KingFlint was my Dad's pride and joy, well, KingFlint *and* Stone Hardaway I should say. He loved Stone like he was his son too."

Stone looked at Bobby. "I am sorry, kid. I should have told you."

Don continued, "Stone was the only one who ever rode KingFlint, he and that horse were unbeatable. It devastated my dad when Stone died, and then when KingFlint was injured in the Derby, well...that was the last straw. Dad retired and hasn't set foot on a track since then."

Bobby just stood there, looking at the two men.

Stone said angrily, "Flint could have won that race, he *should* have won it! Paul had to make a last minute substitution and he chose this idiot who had supposedly been a riding champion in Argentina or somewhere down there. It was his carelessness and refusal to listen to instructions that caused KingFlint to be injured. He had to be pulled up and never finished the race. In fact, he never raced again."

Don said, "The coroner said Stone should have died instantly, but my dad said Stone and KingFlint had chased roses so long that Stone wasn't going to let KingFlint lose his chance at the Derby, even if he had lost his."

Bobby stood there like he was in a trance, until Stone said, "Kid, are you okay?"

Bobby nodded and then he looked at Don Dowd and said, "Are you telling me that you think Stone Hardaway is dead?"

This was like a bad dream.

Don reached over and patted Bobby arm, "Bobby," he said, "I was there, Stone died in the winner's circle at Aqueduct in New York, twenty-five years ago. I'm sorry, I don't know what has happened here, why you think...or who is...well, I have heard rumors over the years that this one or that one has seen Stone. One guy swore he saw him in a crowd at Gulfstream, another thought he saw him right here near the barns, but no one....well, no one until now, has been able, well, has thought they could see *and* talk to him."

Bobby was getting mad, "So what you are saying is, you *cannot* see Stone Hardaway...who is standing right there beside you?"

Don looked again where Bobby pointed, then looked back at Bobby and shook his head. Bobby looked at Stone and Stone smiled a half smile and shrugged.

"You are both a couple of jerks," Bobby shouted

and ran from the room. He ran all the way to the main entrance gate and stopped, bent over, out of breath.

"You sure are out of shape for a skinny kid," Stone said. "You ought to work out, run on the beach. If you are going to be a decent jockey, you need to have plenty of wind and endurance."

Bobby just glared at him and said, "Why did you guys pull that crap on me? Is it a rookie thing or what?" Stone disappeared right before Bobby's eyes. Then he reappeared as quickly as he went.

"I am sorry, Bobby. I don't understand why you are able to see me after all these years and no one else has been able to. Well, someone else did once, but that was a long time ago."

"How did you do that? I mean if you're dead, well how are you here?"

"I am not sure. I haven't been able to find the answer to that one yet."

"I have to go. I think I have lost it. I think I am standing here talking to a...a...ghost or something," Bobby said.

"It's okay kid, I understand." And Stone turned and walked away. Bobby stood where he was for a while and then went to his car and drove home. He went upstairs to his room without speaking to his mother, Craig, or Aunt Iris. Joy followed him up the stairs, but his door was closed and locked.

She knocked softly and said, "Bobby, are you okay?"

"I just need a few minutes, Mom. Please, I just need to be alone."

"Sure honey, but is everything all right? Did something happen at work?"

"No, everything is fine. I just need some time to think." He stayed in his room for the rest of the night. But he didn't sleep.

FOUR

When the sun colored the eastern sky with the first rays of light and color, Bobby stood up and walked to the window. He looked out at the ocean, watching as a freighter seemed to inch along. There was a strong breeze and as Bobby watched the palm trees bending with the wind, he caught sight of Sandy walking on the beach. He smiled as she stood facing the water, her arms behind her back, her head tossed back as if she was burying her face in the early morning sun.

He wished he were standing there with her, holding her, kissing her in the wind and in the mist of the crashing waves. Bobby could just watch and envy the water as she waded in its foamy waves. He reluctantly turned away from the window after a few minutes when the phone rang and his Aunt Iris called up to him that it was Don Dowd. Bobby wasn't sure how to deal with Don Dowd; he wasn't sure how he felt after yesterday. Don must think he was a lunatic.

Stone *was* real. He had touched him. He had smelled his after-shave. The horses loved him; they nuzzled him as he fed them peppermints. He had seen him drink a cup of coffee. How could he be a ghost, or a spirit and do all those things? There had to be an answer, and the answer was that Don and Stone were playing a practical joke on him just like the other grooms and hot walkers at Calder had done since he arrived. *But then,* he thought, *how did he do that disappearing and reappearing trick like he did last night? Had to be some kind of magic act.* He went to the phone sure that Don Dowd and Stone Hardaway were together and having a good laugh and they were going to tell him that the joke was over. He picked up the phone and said," Hello." He heard the extension click and knew that Iris had hung up.

"Bobby? Hey, this is Don. I was just checking on you. I wanted to see if you were still planning to come to work today?"

Bobby said quietly, "You mean I still have a job?"

Don Dowd laughed, "Well sure you do. This is a one of those stranger-than-life things that happen sometimes, but we will figure it out, there's always an explanation for everything. I really would like to have you back. In fact, I had called you in my office yesterday to ask you if you were serious about wanting to go to Kentucky with us. I think you can easily start riding, I have never seen anyone learn as quickly as you have.

You are a natural. So, if you want to go, I will help you get your jocks' license, pay you a regular salary until you get some riding jobs, and let you bunk with some of the guys till you can afford to get your own place. How does that sound?"

Bobby was thrilled; this was just what he had always wanted. But he kept waiting for him to say he was sorry about the Stone Hardaway joke. "Don, what about Stone?"

There was silence on the other end and for a moment Bobby was afraid he had hung up.

"When you get here this morning, we will talk about that some more."

Bobby said, "Thank you for the job offer, Don. I can go as soon as I graduate from school in a few weeks." Don told him he had plenty of time, they still had the Gulfstream meet before they would leave. After they hung up, Bobby began to have doubts and worries.

First, he hated to leave Sandy. And he hated to leave his mother, although she was so wrapped up in her romance with Craig that he wasn't sure she would even notice that he was gone. He hated to leave Iris; he had become very fond of her. But he still had concerns about Stone. He wanted him to go to Kentucky too.

"Hey," he yelled at himself, "what are you, weird? You have a father fixation or something?" He dressed and drove to the racetrack and found Stone by the fence in his usual place. He stood beside him for a few minutes and Stone looked at him without speaking. "Don Dowd offered me a job in Kentucky," Bobby said.

"That's great," Stone said.

Bobby looked down at the ground and said quietly, "I hate to leave Sandy."

"She'll wait, and probably not have to wait long."

"I don't want to leave you, Stone. Feels weird to say that but I don't know, I just feel like I can't leave you. Like I am some little kid about to go off and leave his dad."

Stone turned and faced Bobby. "Kid, I gave this a lot of thought last night, there has to be a reason that you can see me and no one else can. So, what I decided was that maybe you can see me because you need me. What I mean is, you need me to teach you. Maybe what I have been hanging around for is the opportunity to pass on what I was given, but it had to be to the right person. I think my reason for being here is to teach you to be a good jockey."

Bobby said, "What are you talking about? You are not still trying to pull that ghost crap on me are you? I am a dumb kid I know, but I also can tell when somebody is alive or dead!"

Stone laughed, "Hey! I know this is hard for you to understand, it's hard for me to understand too. I am the one who is dead! But for some reason, I have been left here to do something and I wasn't sure what it was. Till now, like I just said, to teach you to be a good jockey."

"I don't want to be a good jockey—I want to be a great jockey!"

Stone laughed, "Okay, Okay. I am not sure I was a great jockey, but I was a good one and I can teach you. You have a good mind and you have learned so much already."

Bobby shook his head, "I am going to have to think about this ghost business, it's weird. And it's all well and good that you want to teach me, but I am going to be in Kentucky. How will we work that, osmosis or whatever you call it?"

Stone laughed, "There are several pictures of me on some walls in Kentucky. I can probably still find my way there."

"You mean go *with* me to Kentucky?"

"Sure why not, I always loved Kentucky. You go, I go too—deal?"

Bobby was all smiles, "Shoot, yeah!"

As Don neared the fence, he could see Bobby animatedly talking and he coughed loudly.

Bobby turned around smiling and said, "How long before we go to Kentucky, Don? I am ready!"

"We have a few months yet, and we still have work to do. So I wondered if you were still on the payroll?"

"Oh yes sir, I sure am, sorry. I will get right to work."

"Great," Don said. "See you at the barns in a minute." Don stared at the empty spot beside Bobby and shook his head.

"Better get to work," Bobby said to Stone. "You coming?" While Don stood there, Bobby talked to Stone. Don was not sure how to behave. He shuffled from one foot to the other and then began to wonder if perhaps it was he who was the butt of a practical joke.

Stone smiled as Don squirmed and he said to Bobby, "Later kid, I'll be up there after while." Stone smiled as Bobby and Don walked away. Bobby talked animatedly to Don, while Don kept looking back over his shoulder to make sure there wasn't someone walking behind him. When they reached the barn area, Don went in his office and Bobby started to the barn.

As he walked past Don's door, he came back, stuck his head in, and said, "Can I ask you a question, Don?"

"Sure, Bobby," Don answered. "Come on in. What's on your mind?"

"Will you tell me some things about Stone?"

Don looked at him and realized he was serious, "Like what?"

"What kind of man was he? He said he never married. Did he have a life other than the races?"

Don laughed. "The horses were his passion, but he had a life away from here. He had Angie. She was really his life. They were together a long time. Actually, she's the one you should talk to about Stone, if you really want to know about him."

"Where does she live?" Bobby asked.

"She lives just a few miles from here, still lives in the house they bought. I am surprised you haven't already talked to her."

"Why would I do that? I don't even know who she is. I didn't even know about her."

Don looked at him with a strange smile, "That's funny. She's your girlfriend's aunt."

"Sandy's Aunt Angie?" Bobby asked. "I had no idea."

Bobby shook his head. No wonder Sandy thought she recognized the name when he spoke about Stone to her. She couldn't put them together since the only

Stone she knew of was her aunt's dead boyfriend. Bobby called Sandy from Don's office and asked her to see if Angie would talk to him at her house. He had some questions about Stone.

When Bobby got home that evening, Sandy told him that Angie would be happy to talk to him about Stone. He was to go to her house the following evening. Sandy was surprised when he told her that he wanted to see Angie alone. And he couldn't tell her why; she would think he had lost his mind. And he wasn't sure that he hadn't lost it.

Practical Bobby Tolliver was buying into a ghost story.

. . .

Bobby was nervous all afternoon before seeing Angie. He didn't know what to say to her or how she might respond to him. And he certainly couldn't tell her that he could see Stone. It still didn't seem real to him. Maybe seeing Angie, and where Stone had lived, finding out some personal things about him, would help him get it all clear in his mind. Bobby pulled into the driveway of the attractive house and parked his car. He hoped Stone wouldn't feel like he was going behind his back, but he had so many questions he wanted to ask, and he wasn't sure Stone would answer him if he did ask.

Angie answered the door and Bobby was taken aback by how pretty she was. He didn't know why he was surprised she was so pretty, after all she was Sandy's aunt. And she reminded him a lot of Sandy. Same sweet voice. She had dark hair and the most amazing brown eyes. And she was so tiny, just a tiny wisp of a thing. Angie smiled sweetly and asked him to sit down. Then she waited for him to tell her what type of research he was doing that involved a study about Stone.

Bobby told her he was training to be a jockey and Stone was his idol. He wanted to be as good as he was. "But," he said, "I want to know something about Stone the man."

Angie smiled, "Well, that happens to be my favorite subject. What can I tell you about him?"

Bobby thought to himself, *You can tell me why I am here asking about a ghost.* But what he said was, "Why don't you tell me about some of these pictures?" Bobby glanced around the room and saw picture after picture of Stone. Some in winner's circles, some of Angie and him on fishing trips, at parties, at the beach. There were a number of pictures of him and KingFlint.

Angie showed him around the house and she described the pictures and where they were made. She would smile as she talked about Stone and what they or he was doing in each one.

"KingFlint was a beauty, wasn't he?" Bobby asked.

Angie nodded and said quietly, "Yes, he was special. He was very special to Stone. He loved that horse. Did you know that we were going to get married in the winner's circle at Churchill Downs a few days after the Derby? He was going to be on KingFlint and I was going to be on my mare, Daisy."

Bobby swallowed the lump in his throat with some difficulty.

"We didn't make it to the winner's circle." Bobby could see tears welling in her eyes. "He died before we could be married," she said.

"I'm sorry," he said, "I can't imagine how that must feel."

"I have a lot of bitterness about...well...about racing, about KingFlint, about me."

"Why?" Bobby asked.

She took a deep breath and said, "I was supposed to go that weekend and watch him ride. We were going to stay in New York for a couple more days and relax. He was so tired. He had worked so hard and had invested so much time in that horse, not to mention all of his other rides. He was just exhausted. But, I had a chance to go to a teacher's workshop that weekend. I promised him when he got back from New York we would take a few days off and drive down to the Keys or up to Georgia, somewhere where there were no horses, no racetracks and no KingFlint, and he could relax. So, I didn't go. He was so disappointed, but he didn't make an issue of it, he just told me to enjoy the workshop and watch the race if I could. He said he would blow me a kiss from the winner's circle. He died in the winner's circle, did you know that? He was there alone, I should have been with him, but I wasn't. He just died and there wasn't anything anyone could do. While he was all alone, I was sitting in a boring workshop 600 miles away. I could have gone to that workshop anytime." She turned her head away and Bobby could see the silent sobs as they wracked her body.

She reached for a tissue on the table and blew her nose. "Sorry," she said, "I have no right to be bitter at anyone, it was my choice, my bad decision. I keep blaming that horse." She laughed bitterly. "And really, there's no one to blame but me."

"He would have died even if you had been there," Bobby said. "You're being there wouldn't have saved him. You can't go on blaming yourself."

"I know that, but he wouldn't have been alone."

"Paul Dowd was there wasn't he? And Don Dowd, weren't they both there?" Bobby asked.

"Yes, Paul loved Stone, and Stone loved the old man. And Stone loved KingFlint. Did you know he got him all the way around that racetrack even though he had that busted artery? Held onto that horse and got him across the finish line. The doctors were amazed—they swore that there was no way he didn't die instantly. None of us were shocked though. Stone had this relentless determination to get KingFlint into that winner's circle. He was getting cheated out of chasing roses, but he sure as heck wasn't going to let his horse lose his shot."

Bobby said, "Don Dowd told me that story and it just blows my mind."

"Yes," Angie said. "He was the most incredible man."

Bobby stood up, thanked her for her time, and started for the door. "Thank you for sharing your memories, I hope they haven't made you too sad."

"All of my memories of Stone are good ones—just the thought of him makes me happy."

"I am surprised that you never married anyone else, you are really pretty. If you don't mind my saying so."

Angie smiled, "Thank you Bobby, that's very sweet. But after Stone, well everyone else seemed sort of mediocre. Quite frankly, I never met anyone that I thought could carry his boots."

Bobby said, "I know what you mean."

Angie said, "I miss him everyday of my life. Some days I can see his picture and feel like a knife has gone in my heart. And some days are better. I only think about him a hundred times or so."

Bobby smiled, "I know how you must feel. I feel that way about Sandy."

She smiled at him and took his hand, "You have made our little Sandy very happy. And I have never known my brother to walk around with a such a huge smile until your mother came along. We are very lucky that you came into our lives."

Angie started to close the door behind Bobby and he stopped suddenly and asked, "Will you not think I am crazy if I tell you something?"

"Well," Angie said with a smile. "That just depends."

And so Bobby stepped back inside and told Angie about meeting Stone at the fence at Calder. He told her about how Stone was training him, and how everyone else thought he had lost his marbles. She cried as she listened, and Bobby was afraid she would hate him for telling her.

"Come sit down," Angie told Bobby, and they walked over to the sofa. "Please finish telling me your story."

When he was through, she looked at his face and smiled. "I believe you Bobby. I saw him too…not long after he died."

"You did?" Bobby asked.

"Yes, and I could feel his presence a lot, just a sense that he was near me. I would come home from school and sit in his chair and I could just sense him in the room with me. It gave me great comfort to know he was still here. Sometimes he would touch my cheek or stroke my hair. "But, she sadly began. "One morning I got to school a few minutes earlier than normal. I spoke to the principal as I walked by, went to the teacher's lounge and got a cup of coffee and went to my classroom. I opened the door and laid my things on the desk. I could just feel someone in the room with me and I looked up—and there was Stone. He was sitting at the back of the room in a student's desk, just sitting there, smiling at me."

"What did you do?" Bobby asked.

"I screamed," Angie said sadly. "I screamed and ran from the room. Can you believe I did that? The love of my life sitting there waiting for me, and I screamed and ran away." Angie buried her face in her hands and sobbed. Bobby sat quietly and let her cry. "Stone was the only man I ever loved. He wasn't just my world, he was my universe, Bobby. How could I run away?"

"It caught you off guard, Angie, that's easy to understand."

"Well, easy to understand or not, I never saw his face again. That face I love so much. Those eyes...you could swim in Stone's eyes. I loved for him just to look at me. But, I ran away. And then, I never saw his face again. Sometimes I still feel him in this room. And there are times when I walk into the room and I swear I can smell his aftershave. But, oh I long to see his face again."

Bobby reached over and patted her hand.

"Tell him that I love him Bobby, and ask him to forgive me for not being there with him when he needed me. Will you please tell him that for me?"

Bobby nodded. "I'll tell him."

When he got in his car, Bobby felt like he had not breathed in two hours. He felt tired and depressed.

As he drove home, he thought about going off to Kentucky and leaving Sandy. He thought about how she would feel if something happened to him and she wasn't there. He thought about Stone and Angie, the great love they had shared, and how Angie's life had been shattered by his death. And he thought about Stone and now he understood the sadness in his eyes.

He felt tears burn his face and he cried all the way home.

After Bobby drove away, Angie sat down in the floor with a silver frame that held Stone's picture. She leaned with her back against the couch and stared at his face. Her finger ran along the curve of his cheek and chin. His eyes were crinkled in a smile and she could almost hear his voice. She thought back to the day they had this picture made and it made her laugh out loud.

He had needed a new picture for the programs at the racetracks. The only picture they had was about ten years old and he hated it. One of the people at Churchill Downs told him that he should see this photographer and get new ones made, and he grudgingly agreed to go, if Angie would go with him.

She had told Stone she thought they should have their picture made together while they were at it and surprisingly, Stone readily agreed.

At the photographer's shop, they acted silly and joked with the receptionist. There was a display with all kinds of goofy hats and Stone and Angie tried them all on each other. An elderly couple was in the waiting room, there to have their picture taken for their fiftieth wedding anniversary. Angie thought they looked so sweet as they sat there holding hands. Stone told her that they would come back to this shop when they were celebrating their fiftieth wedding anniversary and have their pictures made again. Another promise he didn't get to keep.

When he sat down to pose for the picture, he made a sour face, and Angie laughed. She told him that people would think he hated his job with that look. So, he got this silly, sweet look on his face and the photographer snapped the picture. He took a number more of a serious, solemn Stone, but the one Angie loved was that first one. Stone had tried for years to get it away from her and trash it; but after a while, it became their private joke and he would threaten to burn it, but all in good fun. She loved that expression. That was the Stone she knew. The one that people never got to see. And she was glad that she had that part of him all to herself.

He was an incredible rider. He loved the horses. It was almost like he had a personal relationship with each one. He said he was nothing more than their steering wheel, and he always gave the horse the credit when they won a race. He liked what he did, and the public loved him. He was friendly to the crowds, always acknowledging them as he came on to the racetrack, or after he had won a race. He never tried to ignore the people that wanted autographs, especially the kids. He became even more popular because of his accessibility. He wanted the crowds near them up to a point.

Some horses were very shy and the crowds made them even more skittish. He always let the horse decide how much crowd-time they got. KingFlint was one of those rare horses that actually loved the crowds. *The more the merrier*, Stone would say. He was a big gentle horse, but a very professional one. He came to the track for one thing, and that was to race. Stone always said KingFlint reminded him of a construction worker, coming to work every day carrying his silver lunch bucket, ready for the day's labor.

Maybe that was one reason Stone loved to ride him. He just did his job, acted happy to be there and then went back to the barn a winner. All in a day's work, a job well done. But Angie knew there was more to it than that. There was Paul Dowd.

Paul was a strange man, and Angie hadn't really liked him very much. He had no personality, no sense of humor, and she really thought if he hadn't had Stone riding for him, he probably wouldn't have been a very successful trainer. Stone could turn a plow horse into a Derby prospect. (At least that was what the Daily Racing Form had written about him.) What Angie found strange about Paul was his attitude toward his son Don.

He took Stone under his wing and treated him like he was a king. But he acted as if his own son was nothing more than a stable hand. Angie had seen the pain in Don Dowd's eyes more than once. And it was just a wonder that he didn't despise Stone. She could sense a little resentment, but not what she thought she would have felt if it had been her father treating her the way Paul treated him. Don loved his father and you could tell that he wished he could do something to make him love him. But it was Stone who got all the admiration from Paul Dowd. Angie wondered if Don was happier now that he had the successful training business, his breeding business, and his father out of the picture. And maybe he even felt that way about Stone too.

She liked Don's wife Karen and always thought those two could make it just fine if that old man was gone. He made Angie feel uneasy, not just because of his ill temper and maltreatment of his own son, but because she always felt there was just something fishy about him. And she had big doubts about his training ability. One time in the stands, she overheard a couple of trainers talking about him. They didn't realize who she was, or if they did know, they just weren't paying attention.

One trainer told the other that there had been rumors of an investigation of Dowd's stock. This was before they had accurate means to test horses for drugs. He told his pal that a jockey who rode one of his horses said that the horse was breathing like he had been running for hours when they brought him to the paddock. The dead give-away of a horse injected with a speed-enhancing drug.

Angie tried to talk to Stone about it, but he wouldn't hear anything bad said about Paul Dowd. He felt he owed his career to him.

Paul had good horses. But they weren't all as well bred and well behaved as KingFlint. She had seen Stone fall a number of times from skittish horses, and every bad fall he had taken had been from one of Paul Dowd's animals. When she tried to talk to him about it, he acted shocked that she would even consider it Paul's fault that an animal had broken down, or was nervous and went out of control on the track.

Stone just had a blind spot when it came to Paul.

There were times when Angie had even considered asking a friend to see if there wasn't someone who could test his horses and make sure they weren't being hyped up on something. And then when he had his fall in the Arlington race, she took the bull by the horns and went to see Don Dowd.

She never told Stone about it.

Angie knew nothing about horses and the way they

should act. But she had seen Stone on that horse before, that PleasantDream. And just a gut instinct or woman's intuition, call it whatever, she knew something was wrong with that horse. And she knew Don Dowd knew. When she confronted him about it, he tried to act as if he knew nothing. But she could see right through his act. When he finally admitted that he did know what his dad had been up to, he was almost relieved that she figured it out. And she was happy to find out that Don felt like she did, that it was very wrong for his father to do to the horse *and* to the jockeys that rode them. Not to mention that it was highly unethical, illegal, and would have ruined Paul forever.

Don asked her to give him a chance to make his father do what was right. And she promised not to tell the authorities if he did. What she didn't know was that Don had already decided that he wasn't going to allow his father to get away with the illegal drugging. Then when Angie came to see him about her suspicions, and Paul Dowd got KingFlint; that made Don's decision very easy. There was no way he would allow his father to drug up this wonderful horse.

Angie began to watch the horses carefully. She became an expert on how a horse should look in the paddock, and how a doped horse would look. And from that day on, she felt certain that Paul Dowd was not using the drugs on his horses at all.

Then Stone had his aneurysm and it was a moot point. It certainly wasn't Paul Dowd's fault that he had died. Angie thought Paul was a strange, greedy man; but he certainly hadn't killed Stone.

Angie found it hard not to think about Bobby Tolliver being able to see and talk to Stone.

That meant Stone was still around. Her first instinct was to run to Calder and roam around the barns until he saw her and showed himself again. But she couldn't do that. Perhaps there was a reason she couldn't see him after the classroom incident. She still remembered the look on his face. She could see him sitting there smiling at her like it was as natural as could be. And when she screamed, the expression on his face changed to absolute sorrow. She would give anything if she could take that day back, and start all over. In fact, she wished she could start her life over, beginning right at the part where she met and fell in love with Stone.

Angie just hoped that Bobby would give Stone her message. She wished so much she could just see him and hold him again before she died. She could see her reflection in the glass of the picture frame. She looked gray and pale. This disease was gaining on her. The doctors had hoped she would be able to survive another year, but the last visit she had made to the oncologist had taken away the last few threads of hope. He was going to try chemotherapy, even though it had not been successful in other cases like hers. She hadn't even cared until now. If she could live long enough to see Stone again, then she could die happy.

She put the picture back on the end table and went to bed. All night she struggled to stay on a horse that was bucking and trying to throw her. And when she finally got the horse to the barn in her dream, someone was standing in a dark corner of the barn with a huge needle and an ominous grin on his face. She awoke with a start and sat up in bed. Her face was beaded with sweat and she was very thirsty. She got up and went to the kitchen for a glass of water and as she walked by the end table, she could see the picture of Stone had been moved and was now lying on his chair. She looked around and quietly went back to bed. As she turned out the bedside lamp she said, "I love you, my darling." She fell asleep and rested well all the rest of the night.

. . .

With the school change, and the extra credits he had earned, Bobby would be finished with school at midterm and he planned to work fulltime until Sandy graduated in the summer. Since Sandy still had the rest of the spring semester to go, there was not going to be a graduation party. Bobby wanted to wait and share the special time with Sandy when she graduated. Besides, he reasoned with the family, he had a lot of work to do at Gulfstream.

The meet was a few days away from starting and Don Dowd surprised Bobby with a gift. It was the paperwork to get his jockey license.

"Call it a belated Christmas present," he told him.

Bobby was so excited, and he couldn't wait to tell Stone. But Stone didn't act like he was excited about it at all. In fact, Stone told him that he should wait a few months.

"You have learned a lot, but we still have a lot of work to do. I just don't want you out there getting hurt."

Bobby got mad and as he stormed off he said, "I have worked hard and Don Dowd, who is a *good* trainer, thinks I am ready! Why don't you just admit that you are jealous?" A number of people were standing around, intently watching as Bobby held a one-sided argument. Don Dowd came out of his office and ushered Bobby away from the crowd.

"What are you doing Bobby? Are you crazy? I let it slide that you think you can talk to a dead jockey, but I can't have an employee of mine standing in front of people carrying on an imaginary conversation. People will think you are nuts, or even worse, that you are on drugs! Now you need to get a grip!"

Bobby took a deep breath and said, "Sorry, Don. But Stone made me mad."

Don shook his head and frowned, "Why?"

"He doesn't want me to get my jock license yet. He says I have a ways to go before I am ready."

"I see, Don said. Did he...uh...say why?"

"No, he made me mad and I wasn't listening to him."

"Bobby," Don began. "Didn't you tell me that everything you have learned you have learned from Stone?" Bobby nodded. "Well, now understand that I don't really believe that Stone talks to you, but doesn't it make sense that if he has taught you everything you know so far, that he might have a reason for not wanting you to make that big a move just yet?"

"But you think I can do it." Bobby muttered.

"I want you to be able to ride when you felt ready. You would have that paperwork done so if you had the opportunity, you'd be able to go for it. I wasn't pushing you onto the track yet."

Stone had been standing inside the door listening.

Bobby looked up at Stone and said, "Sorry, Stone."

Stone smiled at him, "What the heck, kid. We had better get to work then. I can see you won't be sidelined long."

Don looked at Bobby's face. "You okay?"

"Yes sir," Bobby replied. "I think I must be under more stress than I thought, but I had no right to yell like that."

"Okay, Bobby," Don said. Bobby and Stone walked out of the office and people stared at him. But he smiled and ignored them. He and Stone chatted as they went back to work.

FIVE

As they walked away from the barns, Bobby asked Stone about some of the big races he had been in. Stone was always happy to talk about his races. But today he thought that this kid had better hear about some of the bad races, the ones that ended with him being on his back in a hospital bed, or off work with an injury for weeks, taking therapy so he could not just ride, but walk again.

Bobby was all ears for anything Stone had to say, so as he worked, Stone talked. He told him about the Arlington Million. The race that put him out of commission for five months, and killed his good friend Armenio Vasquez.

Stone said, "I loved Arlington Park in Chicago. This was at the old track, before it burned down. The race was a turf race, the eighth on the card that day. I had ridden in two other races, the Big D and a high allowance race. All of the horses were trained by Paul Dowd, but two of them had the same owner. The allowance horse, PettyLarceny, and the three-year-old stakes placed, PleasantDream.

"PleasantDream was anything but a pleasant dream. He was a handful in the paddock, on the track, and in the barn. He bit other horses so he had to be kept away from the others during the post parade. I had ridden him twice before and knew he always acted the fool, so I was prepared for his antics. Usually a good pop on the side his head would bring him around.

"Another horse in the race, JillyNilly, was a nice bay gelding from Tom Arseneaux's barn and was just as big a screwball as PleasantDream. And they were side by side in the gate in post positions seven and eight. PleasantDream was number seven. The handlers kept PleasantDream back from the gate till everyone else had loaded. As they tried to put JillyNilly, who was being ridden by Armenio Vasquez in the gate, the horse tried to rear up and in the process, kicked the lead pony.

"It was all Armenio could do to stay on when JillyNilly started acting up. I heard Armenio cussing in Spanish and I yelled at him to give the horse a pop on the head. Armenio said something about the only pop this nag needed was a pop from a large caliber handgun; all the jockeys laughed. They loaded PleasantDream and the gates opened quickly. It was a good, clean break from the gate; I took up on my horse and let the early speed set up for their run. PleasantDream liked to be just off the lead or about a length off of the speed especially if there was a speed horse in the race.

"The speed horse was JillyNilly. Speed horses usually take off fast; and run as fast as they can for as long as they can. Usually a speed horse has success if they are the only speed in the race. If there is other speed, a duel usually develops and the late runners, or the closers as they are called, can come running late and pass the tiring speed horses. JillyNilly had the lead pretty much to himself, no one wanted to run with him this early. Armenio tried to slow him down and relax him as they made the first turn, but he was determined to be running as fast as he could. One advantage to being lone speed is being able to slow down the pace so the horse doesn't have to work hard going so blazing fast throughout the entire race. Unfortunately, JillyNilly didn't want to slow down, and very few horses can keep up such a frantic pace."

Bobby interjected, "I have noticed that about speed horses."

Stone continued. "The horses that ran in mid pack started gaining on JillyNilly and I am sure Armenio knew he was in trouble. The horse could not sustain the pace he was setting. They had gone a quarter mile in .21 and .4—they were flying. I could see Armenio struggling to get the horse under control.

"But I was having my own hard time with PleasantDream, who wanted to take a shortcut over the mid field fence and go back to the barn. It was a battle to keep him on the track. The last time I looked at

Armenio, I saw him yelling at the horse, trying to slow him down. The next thing I saw was the horse hit the ground and Armenio fly over the horse's head. The two horses behind him stepped on him and fell, taking their jockeys for a ride in the grass. I tried to guide PleasantDream off the rail and out of the way of the accident but he was spooked, and he bolted and made a sharp left turn. I went to the right as my horse went to the left. I went flying head first on to the turf, and even though the three horses behind me made every effort to avoid me, only one of them missed me.

"I heard the screaming fans and the sirens. I heard the track announcer say that five jockeys were down, and two looked seriously injured. He told the crowd that three of the jockeys were sitting up, but Stone and Armenio were lying in the grass not moving. I remember that I couldn't move; I couldn't even breathe. I wanted to move; I wanted to check on Armenio. I saw him fall, and I knew it was bad. I wasn't sure how badly I was hurt, but I hurt all over. The paramedics were trying to talk to me but I could only think about Armenio...and that Angie was going to be so mad at me if I missed our anniversary on Friday. Finally, the thoughts left and there was peaceful sleep.

"The first sound I heard was Angie's voice begging me to open my eyes. I didn't want to open my eyes. I was so tired, and Lord, it hurt to take a breath! When I peeked at her, I saw that she had been crying. That worried me because Angie was not one to cry over anything."

Stone continued, "She was holding my hand." As

Stone told Bobby the story, he could almost feel her small hand in his. "She leaned over and whispered, 'Please tell me that was your last race.' When I asked her why it hurt so bad to breathe, she told me I had punctured a lung, broken my leg, and had other internal injuries.

"I asked about Armenio, but she told me to wait until I felt better and we would talk about it. I was still pretty groggy but I remember thinking that I didn't like the sound of that one bit. I was out for almost a day and a half. The Dowd's hung around the hospital and there were reporters for the local paper and the Racing Form waiting to see me. One of them managed to slip by the drill sergeant of a nurse and get into my room while everyone was out having dinner.

"I remembered seeing the guy before. He was a staff writer for the Racing Form, and I had always thought he was a pretty good guy. Until that day. He leaned over the bed and asked me how I was feeling. Then he made the mistake of asking me how I felt about Armenio dying in the race.

"Lucky for him I wasn't able to get out of that bed, but he had leaned too close so I grabbed him by the tie and pulled him down to where we were face to face, noses touching. I yelled at him, 'Get out of here, you lying pig!' It hurt to yell, it still hurt to breathe, but I swear if I could have, I would have strangled him. The guy was yelling for help and a nurse ran in and physically threw him out the door of my room.

"I asked the nurse to come closer to my face so I

could talk to her. I asked her if what he said was true, that Armenio was really dead, and she said, 'He never regained consciousness. The fall broke his neck, it was very quick.'

"It took me a long time to get over Armenio's death. He had a family, three little kids, and a wife who spoke very little English. Angie and I did everything we could to help them until they were able to get back to the Dominican Republic where their family lived."

Bobby was hanging on every word.

Stone said, "There have been others too, but that was the worst one. I almost did quit racing after that. Not just because of my injury but because of the danger. But, it's what I do, so I just became a lot more cautious and careful. People would think I wasn't trying sometimes because I wouldn't force a horse when they just could *not* run any faster. I didn't think it was worth me or a horse dying just to win a pointless race. My point here, Bobby, is that no matter how good—or great—a jockey you are, you are going to get hurt. It's just a matter of time. Horses take bad steps. Another horse can take a bad step and cause your horse to fall. Sometimes in tight quarters during a race, horses can clip heels and cause your horse to fall. The horse can get spooked and do something that would be totally out of character and make you fall. Whatever the circumstances, you *will* fall somewhere along the line. What other business do you know that has an ambulance follow you around while you do your job?"

Bobby laughed. "Well, you have a point there. Why did you go back to racing?"

"Paul Dowd had me and Angie come up to Kentucky for a visit, and he showed me KingFlint. I knew I had to ride him."

I am in a real dilemma, Bobby thought as he listened to the rest of Stone's story. *I haven't told Stone about my visit to Angie yet…the longer I wait, the less sure I am about how to talk to him. This is the first time I've heard him mention her, but I don't know how he'll react if he knows I have been to see her. Maybe I should tell Sandy first. She'll know what to do.*

. . .

Bobby and Sandy had a standing dinner date every Friday evening. Tonight he told her they were going to their favorite diner across the street from Gulfstream. It was an old-time fifties-type diner with great food.

They asked for their favorite booth in the back. Once they were seated, Sandy said, "Okay, out with it."

"You aren't supposed to know me that well yet, not until we have been married about ten years," he laughed.

"You can never play poker," Sandy told him. "You have such an open face."

"Oh great," Bobby laughed. "That was my backup career choice." He was quiet for a minute, took her hands in his, and started to tell her about Stone. The waitress interrupted them with her chitchat and, after she took their order, he tried again.

"You know me pretty well, Sandy, but I have been keeping a secret from you." She looked puzzled. "Remember me telling you about Stone and how much help I was getting?"

She nodded.

"Well, Stone, ummm, Stone is not real. No that's not what I mean to say, of course he's real, but you see, Stone, well..."

Sandy said, "What? What about Stone?"

"Remember the man Angie was going to marry?"

"Stone? Wait a minute, Bobby. Are you saying that Angie's Stone is really alive?"

"No, not exactly."

"Well, what exactly? What has your Stone got to do with Angie's Stone?"

"It's the same man," Bobby said and then he looked down.

"What?" Sandy almost shouted and some of the other people around looked over at them.

"Stone is a...a...ghost, I guess you'd say. Or a spirit, not sure what the official name is. But he's definitely not uhhhh...well like you and me."

"Bobby, you are scaring me. What are you talking about?"

Bobby told her the entire story, even what Angie had told him about seeing Stone right after he died. She stared at him a long time before she answered.

"So you think you can see and talk to the same man, is that what you're saying? A dead man," she added.

Bobby just nodded.

"Bobby, that's so not funny!"

"Not supposed to be funny, it's the truth."

Sandy was quiet again. The waitress brought their sandwiches. Sandy pushed her potato salad around her plate and never touched her sandwich. Bobby felt a great weight off his chest as he gobbled down his sandwich.

"Angie asked me to tell Stone something for her, and I haven't had the nerve to tell him yet. I was hoping you would tell me whether I should tell him, and how I should say it," Bobby said between bites.

"What are you supposed to tell him?"

"That she still loves him, and that she is sorry for not being in New York when he died. Did you know she was supposed to go with him to that race?"

"No," Sandy said quietly.

"He died during the race, and she feels guilty because she chose to stay in town and go to a workshop."

Sandy asked Bobby, "Did she tell you she has cancer?"

Bobby, with his fork in mid air, stopped and stared at Sandy, "What did you say?"

"Angie has cancer. It is terminal."

Bobby took a deep breath and choked back a sob. "How danged unfair is that?" And he pounded the table.

Sandy studied his face. "You really believe what you are telling me, don't you?"

"It's true honey," he said. "Stone thinks that he has been hanging around all this time waiting for someone to come along that he can teach and pass on the gift he was given. He thinks I can be as good as he was, and that's the reason I can see him and no one else has been able to. It had to be the right person."

Sandy shook her head. "This is crazy," she said.

"Do you think I should tell Stone about going to see Angie?"

"Yes. I think you should honor her request and tell...uh...tell him what she asked you to tell him."

"Ok," Bobby said. "I will." They drove home in silence. Bobby tried to hold Sandy's hand, but she sat with her hands folded in her lap, staring out the passenger side window.

When he pulled in her driveway, Bobby started to open his door to walk her to the front door. But she opened her door herself and said quietly, "I am tired. I will talk to you later. Goodnight." And she dashed in the house, closed the door, and turned off the porch light.

Bobby sat in the driveway for a few minutes and thought about going to the door and trying to talk to her, but he decided he would wait and try tomorrow after she had time to think about everything. Reluctantly, he backed out and drove the two doors down to his house.

The morning was gray and damp, just like Bobby's spirits. Even the ocean looked depressed. Bobby didn't care whether he opened his eyes or not. He could have stayed in bed with the weight of the world on his shoulders. But he sat up on the side of the bed and rubbed his head. He folded his hands between his knees and stared at the wall decorated with pictures of Stone that

Don had given him, and the posters of Lafitte Pincay and Jerry Bailey, two of his favorite jockeys.

"Man," he said to the wall. "This is a real mess." He heard someone knock on the front door, his aunt's voice, a tap on the door of his room.

"Bobby?" It was Sandy. He quickly put on his pants and opened the door. She walked in without being asked and said, "I haven't slept all night."

"Me either," he said.

"I have a hard time believing that Stone is alive, or is here in some form, but I can tell that you do, and I can tell you are sincere when you talk about him. I know you have been working very hard and someone has been helping you, and I just know that if the man I love thinks he can see a ghost, well then darn it, it's the truth!"

Bobby said nothing, he just walked over to Sandy and pulled her close to him and held her. He stroked her hair and kissed her ear.

"Marry me, Bobby," she said. "Please, just marry me. Let's get married today."

Bobby didn't have to be asked twice. He packed a bag, and sent Sandy home to pack. He called the track and told Don Dowd that he was going to need to be off for a couple days; and he went over to Sandy's house and the two of them drove away.

They married in quaint little Baptist Church in a nondescript town in Central Florida, then drove back to Dania Beach and stayed two nights at the Springtown Suites. Bobby called Craig Wagner and told him they had gotten married; he didn't want Sandy to have to tell him. He figured he would scream and yell, and Bobby thought he should be the one to have to listen to it instead of Sandy.

Surprisingly, Craig was not as angry as he had supposed he would be. He told Bobby that he had always known they would get married, he just wished they would have waited until Sandy had graduated. Bobby assured him she would finish school, and would still be able to go to college if she wanted. What he failed to tell him was that he was going to Kentucky in a couple months and he was taking his bride with him.

When they got home, Aunt Iris had already planned a reception for them and had bought them matching wedding rings as her gift to them.

The reception was fun and many of his friends from the track came. Neighbors and strangers alike were there, Sandy assured him some were her Dad's clients and friends. Everyone was upbeat and happy. It was a great party.

Bobby walked out of the kitchen into the living room with some ice for the bar and stopped dead in his tracks. Angie was sitting on the couch, and Stone was standing right behind her. He had his hand on her shoulder, listening to her talk to the lady sitting on the couch beside her. He looked up, saw Bobby, and waved. Bobby waved and went to Sandy and said, "Do you see Angie?"

She looked around the room and smiled, "Yes there she is, talking to Ms. Glickman. I wonder who that guy is with her, he sure looks familiar."

Bobby said quietly, "What guy?"

"Duh, Bobby, the one standing behind her with his hand on her—" her hand flew to her mouth. "Oh, no, Bobby, is...is...that—?"

Bobby nodded. Sandy turned and raced from the room. Bobby followed her.

"Hey, hey, it's okay," he said.

She buried her face in his shoulder. "But how...how can I see him? I knew that face, all those pictures of him at Angie's house. I thought I would recognize him anywhere....if....if..."

"It's got to be love that makes you be able to see him." Bobby pulled Sandy back and looked at her face. "You can see him through those beautiful eyes of love." And they stood quietly for a minute until Iris came looking for them and scooted them back out with their guests.

After the party hullabaloo was over, the next question was where they would stay, and Iris won the argument and put them in the bigger guest room in her house. Bobby told Sandy not to get too used to it. They were leaving in a couple months and would have their own home.

. . .

Joy Tolliver cried for hours when she heard about the wedding. She had always hoped Bobby would go to college. Now, she just couldn't see that happening.

Both Craig and Iris tried to reassure her. Finally Iris said, "Bobby has his own road to walk, Joy. You can only stand by and wave him on. He has a lot going for him, and now he has love, you just can't ask for much more than that."

Joy couldn't argue with her older sister's logic.

When Stone saw Bobby at the track the next day, he laughed, "Nice party last night. You weren't kidding about getting married were you?"

"So, did you know all the time that Angie was Sandy's aunt?" Bobby asked.

"Not till you said something about Craig and Sandy. I always knew Craig. Of course, Sandy wasn't born yet. Craig and his wife were still newlyweds and they used to hang out with us a lot. I never really cared much for him, not sure why, he just reminded me of a used car salesman. Couldn't stand his wife."

"He's a good guy," Bobby said. "And yes, I know that Sandy's mother had some emotional problems or something. Sandy hasn't seen her in nine years. She just got up one day and walked away, and no one has heard from her since."

Stone nodded, "That's hard to figure a mom doing to a kid isn't it? Sandy seems very nice, and she's pretty, like her Aunt Angie. What does she see in a string-bean kid like you?" And Stone laughed.

Bobby said, "She saw you with Angie last night. She asked me who you were. I couldn't believe that she could see you."

Stone was surprised too.

"I think it's because of love, our love for each other and her love for Angie."

"You may have something there kid," Stone said.

"Angie is dying Stone." Bobby just blurted it out.

Stone turned around and looked at him. "What are you talking about?"

"She has terminal cancer."

"No, that's not possible. She looks great—she looks perfect," Stone said.

"She's getting worse by the day, but Sandy said that last night she looked good for the first time in a long time."

Stone was quiet.

"I went to see Angie," Bobby said. "I had questions about you. I wanted to know who you were when you were....well.....when you were here."

"And?" Stone asked.

"I hope that Sandy and I always have the kind of love that you two had."

Stone smiled a sad smile. "I do too kid. I do too."

"Angie asked me to give you a message."

"You told her that you can see me?"

"Yes."

"What was the message?"

"She has loved you everyday of her life. And she wants you to forgive her for not being in New York with you."

Stone looked at the ground. "Did she tell you about me showing up in her classroom?"

"Yes."

"I knew then that I had to let her go, let her find her way and make a life for herself without me."

"But you didn't let her go. You have touched her hair, or sat in the same room with her, haven't you?"

"Yes, but how did you know that?"

"She told me. You thought you were doing her a favor, but you weren't. She never got over you, and you never got over her."

Stone had tears in his eyes.

"You know what she is the saddest about, Stone?"

Stone shook his head.

"That she never saw your face again. After you startled her in school that day, she has never seen your face again. And it has broken her heart."

"She has pictures."

Bobby mumbled under his breath, "A lot of good a picture does." Stone started to walk away. "Where are you going?"

Stone said nothing, just shook his head and walked off. Bobby watched him walk away. His shoulders seemed bent under a terrible weight.

SIX

Angie sat at her dressing table, staring in the mirror as she brushed her long dark hair. She leaned her head back, closed her eyes, and brushed the back of her hair. When she opened her eyes, she gasped. Stone stood behind her.

He took the hairbrush and began to brush her hair. Their eyes met in the mirror and he smiled at her and said, "I always loved brushing your hair, remember?"

She nodded, reached back and took his hand. He laid the brush on the table as she stood up. He took her in his arms and held her.

"Stone," she said in a choked whisper.

"Bobby told me that Sandy saw me standing behind you at the party last night. Did you know I was there?"

She shook her head. "No, not last night, but I have

felt you with me other times. It's what keeps me going, thinking that you might be here when I come home."

"I am so sorry, Angie. Sorry for dying on you, for ruining the life we had planned."

"Oh Stone," she sobbed, "I am the one who should be sorry. I should have been with you in New York."

"Who could have known something would happen? I never blamed you for not being there. It was selfish of me to want you to come every time I raced. You had your own career."

"No," she said. "It wasn't selfish. I *should* have been with you."

"I knew you would be at the Derby, and I thought we would have plenty of time to go back to New York or wherever we wanted to go. I don't want you to feel guilty anymore."

"I am sick, Stone. Did the kids tell you?'

Stone nodded.

"Will you stay with me tonight? Just sit with me and hold me again?"

"Angie," Stone said as he brushed her hair away from her face. "I have always been here, and I will always be with you."

Angie and Stone sat on the couch. He leaned back with her in his arms and they talked of the past. They laughed and cried together at the memories.

"Sometimes memories are all we have," Angie told him. "Even though I have grieved for you all these years, longing for what might have been, the memories we made together have kept me alive. If I hadn't had

Craig and Sandy here, I don't think I would have cared one way or the other whether I did live or die. And knowing that you were here with me in spirit made life worthwhile. I thought about selling this house, it's so big and empty without you, but I couldn't part with it because there is too much of you here."

She told him she was getting very tired and was ready to go to bed. She lay with her head on his shoulder and studied his profile. She rubbed her fingers across his cheek and swam with delight in the eyes she loved.

She smiled as she told him, "This sure beats just looking at your picture."

She fell asleep right before dawn. He lay with her for a few more minutes, touching her face and watching her sleep. Then he quietly arose, covered her with the blanket, and left the room.

Angie moaned in her sleep and when she reached across for Stone, he wasn't there. But the smell of his after-shave lingered in her pillow. She pulled it to her, held it to her face, and cried.

Bobby saw Stone in the barns the next morning. He waved at Bobby and smiled.

"We have some work to do this morning," Bobby said.

"No sweat, I will watch while you do it," Stone laughed.

"Gee thanks, you're too kind."

Bobby was washing out the stalls and tossing trash from the barn area. Stone sat on an upside-down box and chewed on a piece of straw. Bobby thought he looked a million miles away.

"Where are you today?" Bobby asked him.

Stone looked at him and said, "I was just thinking about Angie. I went to see her last night."

Bobby stopped and leaned against his rake. "I thought you might. How was everything?"

Stone smiled, "She hasn't changed a bit, she is so beautiful," he said wistfully. "I love her as much today as I did twenty-five years ago. But I sure gypped her out of a happy life."

"How do you figure?" Bobby said.

"Well, we didn't get to marry. She had no children, no other romance or love in her life. So she has just spent twenty-five years mourning for what might have been."

"Seems to me that was her choice," Bobby said. "She said everyone seemed mediocre after you. Sometimes love makes the decision for us Stone."

"I am supposed to be teaching you kid, not the other way around." He laughed and said, "I know one thing, you are one sorry stall-mucker!" And he threw a handful of hay at Bobby.

. . .

The Gulfstream meet was almost over and Don Dowd was getting ready to head to Kentucky. He had already shipped most of his string of horses to the farm in Paris, Kentucky. He had two high allowance horses he was leaving to finish the season at Gulfstream and one stakes-placed horse he wanted to run in the last stakes race of their meet.

He left Bobby and Iggy to take care of the three, and Sam, his assistant trainer, stayed to oversee the operations.

There wasn't as much to do now and that gave Bobby and Stone a lot of time to train with the horses that Don left.

Bobby had not given up on getting the jockey license, but he didn't nag Stone about it either. He trusted him to have him ready to ride like a pro; when that happened, it would be Stone who would tell him to go get the license. He just hoped it wouldn't be long.

He wasn't disappointed.

Stone spent a lot of time gone from the track, and Bobby knew he was with Angie. She was supposed to have started taking chemotherapy but she was too ill to take the medicine. The doctor put her in the hospital, supposedly to build her up so she could take the treatments.

Sandy had been spending a lot of time with her too. She told Bobby she didn't know why they tortured people like that when they knew there was nothing they could do to save them.

In the end, Sandy was right. Angie started hemorrhaging and they rushed her to intensive care and called in the family to be with her during the last hours.

Bobby was supposed to be leaving for Kentucky but he called Don Dowd and told him that he would be delayed. Don understood and Sam and Iggy left Florida with the last horses.

—

Bobby wanted to be with Sandy and Craig, and Stone.

Stone was at the hospital by Angie's side every moment. He held her hand, wiped her face, and whispered to her. She would call his name, he would kiss her face, and she would rest a little.

But it made everyone in the room very sad that she was calling out for Stone.

Craig was beside himself with grief and Joy said that maybe Stone *was* there with her as she faced death.

Only Bobby, and perhaps Sandy, knew that he really was.

Her last words were meant for Stone, "I love you."

Stone told her that he would always love her. "We will be together again my love, I promise you. We will be together again." And he leaned over, kissed her, and said, "I will see you soon, baby. I won't break another promise."

He walked from the room sobbing.

Bobby found him later in an empty, dark waiting room.

"Are you okay, Stone?" he asked.

He cleared his throat and said, "Maybe now she will find peace."

"And what about you, Stone? Are you going to be able to find peace?"

"I hope one day I do, kid, but I have some unfinished business yet."

"And that is...?" Bobby asked.

"You are part of it, I don't know the rest yet, but I will when it happens."

Sandy came to the door of the waiting room and said, "There you are, I was looking for you."

Bobby walked over and took her hand. "Let's get out of here, I know you are exhausted."

Stone said, "I'll see you, kid."

"There will be a memorial service for Angie in a couple days," Bobby said. "As soon as the arrangements are made."

"I said my goodbyes tonight, Bobby. Those services are for the living, not the dead."

As Bobby turned to leave he said, "I am sorry, Stone."

Stone looked up at him and nodded.

They had the memorial service three days later. Many people attended, and Bobby looked all through the crowd for a sign of Stone. But he wasn't there.

After the service as they walked from the gravesite to their cars, people stood around for a few minutes and talked. There was to be visitation at Craig's house and everyone got in their cars and left the cemetery.

Bobby and Sandy had driven their own car, and they were some of the last ones to leave. They sat for a minute while Sandy talked about her aunt. She started to cry. Bobby leaned over to hug her and as he did, something caught his eye.

He turned and looked out the back window and saw a solitary figure standing at the grave. The figure leaned over and placed a single red rose on the pile of flowers, and then turned and walked away. Bobby drove away with tears in his eyes.

SEVEN

It was three days before Bobby saw Stone again. He was beginning to be afraid he was gone for good.

"Well finally," Bobby said. "I was worried about you."

"I am a bad penny. You should have known I would show back up."

"Don wants me in Kentucky in three days. And guess what?"

"What?"

"This two-year-old he is so excited about?"

"Yes?"

"It's a progeny of KingFlint. Guess what the name is? Are you ready for this? FlintRemembered."

Stone was quiet for a minute and then asked, "So it's a colt?"

"Yep."

"Well, how about that. The old boy's going to get another shot at it."

"Whatever happened to KingFlint after he was injured?" Bobby asked. "How did that injury happen anyway?"

And Stone told Bobby about Esteben Escobar and his lousy ride in the Derby.

KingFlint had an outside post position and that was good considering he liked to run from way off the pace. Paul had told Esteben that he wanted him to get KingFlint out of the gate and out of traffic, in order to let the speed horses make their early run and just keep him within striking distance four or five lengths off the leaders.

The horse was bred to run all day; this distance was going to suit him to a tee, and he didn't have to work so hard to stay up with the speed. But as soon as the gate opened, Esteben tried to get Flint out and maneuver a place on the rail. As he headed for the rail, dueling for the lead with a solid speed horse; KingFlint took a bad step, and Esteben had to pull him up. Paul was sure that he had broken his leg and was hoping against hope that the horse wasn't going to have to be put down. Esteben managed to get off the horse and did have the good sense to stay calm and hold onto him until the out-rider and the ambulance arrived.

Paul Dowd made his way over to the vet's office in the barn area to see about his horse. Esteben came running up to him and was yelling about the horse taking a bad step, and Paul had to use every bit of his self-control not to slug the jockey. As soon as he was assured the horse would live, he went back to work.

When the vet told him that the horse would never run again, Paul Dowd was finished with racing.

But before he left, he sent out memos and letters, and talked to every person he met who was in horseracing and did everything he could do to have Esteben Escobar blackballed. He wanted to make sure that the jockey never rode another big race, or at another name track. Stone said that he had heard a number of years ago that he was riding in Colorado or Washington State somewhere.

"KingFlint was a big horse, a real professional. He tried every time you put him on the track. In all the races from the time we started him at two until the Derby, he only lost one race."

Bobby said, "Have any of his other babies raced?"

"Not that I know of. Maybe it's time he got another shot."

Bobby realized that perhaps Stone had a purpose to be there besides teaching him to be a great jockey.

"Hey, Stone, maybe this is what your other job is—teach another kid how to be great."

Stone laughed, "How come I get stuck with a bunch of babies?"

"Oh," Bobby laughed. "It's got to be that paternal instinct."

Stone leaned over, scooped up a handful of dirt, and tossed at Bobby. And they both had a good laugh.

. . .

There were a lot of tears as Bobby and Sandy loaded their car getting ready for the trip to Kentucky.

Craig Wagner talked to both of the kids and gave them a million instructions, then asked to speak to Sandy alone.

Bobby understood and walked over to his house to spend a few minutes with his mother and Aunt Iris. Joy wasn't in the room when he walked in so Aunt Iris, acting as if she had a big secret, called him over to her.

"Bobby, I am so very proud of you, you have worked so hard, and you have such a good head on your shoulders."

"Thank you Aunt Iris. And thank you for letting us live here. I am really gonna miss you."

"Oh pshaw, it was a joy to have you around. I had always wished for a son, and you are more than a person could hope their own kid would turn out to be. So," and she handed him an envelope. "Take this and use it to help cover the expenses when you get started."

"I can't take your money, Aunt Iris."

"Oh shoot, of course you can, and you will, I have more money than good sense and I want you and Sandy to get started on the right foot. Bobby, you follow that dream of yours, don't you let anyone talk you out of it, and don't you let anyone steer you from the right road. Now put that in your pocket and say nothing to your mother about it."

He put the envelope in his shirt pocket, leaned

over, and kissed Iris. "Thank you, he said, we will use it wisely."

Joy walked into the room and Bobby could see she had been crying.

He walked over and hugged her, saying, "Now we will have none of that."

She smiled, "That sounded like something your grandfather would have said."

Bobby laughed, "Yep, I thought you needed something to smile about."

"Hey," he said as he hugged his mom. "You and Craig will be up there in just a few weeks, bringing Sandy's car. You act as if you will never see me again. And besides, you two have a wedding coming up of your own, and by the time we see you, you will be Mrs. Craig Wagner. You have a lot to be happy about."

"You just grew up so fast," she said. "I came here with a boy just a short time ago, and now, here you are married, heading off to a riding career, all on your own. I just feel like the time passed us by too fast."

Bobby nodded, "Time really did go by fast when we got here. Maybe time just moves slower in Kentucky. I hope it does. I want to enjoy every day of my life."

He saw Sandy open the front door.

"There is my pretty little navigator, guess we had better head out while we have some daylight left."

He hugged his mom again, and gave Iris another hug and kiss on the cheek.

"Be careful, Bobby," Iris said.

Joy and Craig walked the kids to the car and held each other as they drove away.

Sandy turned around in her seat and waved. "I felt like I was nine years old again, going off to camp or something."

"Yeah, but they mean well."

Sandy said, "My dad gave us a check for $10,000. I told him I wouldn't take it but he said that was what he had saved to get me started in college."

Bobby handed her the envelope from Aunt Iris. "Aunt Iris gave us that. See what's in it."

Sandy whistled. "There is $3,500 cash and a check for another $20,000."

They looked at each other and laughed. "We can probably buy a house with this." But they agreed they would put it in savings until the perfect house came along. Bobby didn't say anything, but he thought to himself that he knew the perfect house already.

Maybe Bobby and Sandy were married, and maybe they were on the way to start a new job and their life together, but they were still teenagers and this trip was their honeymoon. They stopped at roadside parks and had picnics; they made every tourist trap between Miami, Florida, and Paris, Kentucky.

They had plenty of money and they had plenty of time, and they had a ball.

They took turns driving, they sang duets to the music on the radio, they stopped and made love, and they talked and made plans.

Florida seemed far away as they crossed the state line into Kentucky.

. . .

Bobby drove to the Dowd's farm. He had not yet met Don Dowd's wife Karen and he and Sandy liked her immediately.

She and Don were excited about the young couple coming to Kentucky and they took them under their wing and insisted they stay in the guesthouse until they could find a place to live.

Karen and Don had been married for eighteen years. They only had one child, a son who would have been sixteen. He was born with severe birth defects and had died when he was four years old.

They never tried to have other children. Karen thought that it might have been fear that kept them from getting pregnant again. No one was able to explain what caused little Mark to be born so ill, and without a guarantee that it would not happen to another child, they just never tried again.

They had each other and their animals and that was enough for them.

The years were mostly happy. Karen was a devoted wife and she and Don loved each other very much. They worked hard together and when Don had to be on the road, Karen tried to tag along, but she chose her trips with care. Someone had to run their farm, and they never trusted anyone with long-term operations except each other. Karen's saddest moments, except for the loss of their son, were knowing Don's feelings of failure with the horses. She and Don talked about these things a million times. They had a wonderful horse standing at stud, yet the last three colts he sired had all died of the colic. It was so depressing. They had mortgaged their home to buy KingFlint from his dad and the partners in the syndicate that owned him.

Don had wanted a big horse, and he got it with KingFlint. His fillies had been spectacular, but the colts were sickly and unable to live past their second year. And as hard as Don tried, he couldn't figure out why.

Paul Dowd, Don's father, was a bitter man. He blamed Don for his misfortunes and Don could never tell anyone why his father was so angry with him. Angie had been the one person who had figured it out after Stone was injured in the Arlington Million. She came to see him, and he didn't want to admit that his dad was drugging his horses, but she could tell he was lying. He made a deal with her that he would make sure he never did it again, if she wouldn't say anything and ruin his dad's reputation and career. She agreed to go along with Don, but she told him that she would be watching.

KingFlint had been his father's big hope. His Derby horse. From the time they bought him and started training him, he had never let them down. He had lost only one race and that was a fluke. A horse had fallen in front of him as he was making his run from off the pace, and KingFlint had jumped the fallen horse and rider. He looked very much like a steeplechase horse. It was a gallant move on the track, but in doing so, he had lost all chance of winning a race he would have won easily. Stone had managed to stay on and as they approached the crowd after the race, they received a standing ovation. It was the only race KingFlint ever lost, until the Derby.

KingFlint's only jockey had been Stone Hardaway. No one else had ever even worked him over the track. Stone was just a young man when he first rode for Paul Dowd. He was a little arrogant and brash and Paul loved that about him. Stone thought he was good, and he *was* good. He gave the impression that he was the best ever, and he set out to *be* the best ever. Paul Dowd saw through the façade and into the heart of the kid they called Stone Face. He wanted him to have a chance to be the best, so he made him his main rider and the kid went about the business of being the best ever.

In a very short time, he was leading rider in the country and he never slowed down. He tried to win on every horse he rode whether it was a Derby prospect or a $5,000 claiming horse. The thing people loved about him was that Stone loved the horses. He loved what he did. He wouldn't ride a horse hard if he got the feeling that something wasn't right with it. He saved a lot of injuries by not being a bully. The trainers and owners loved him, the horses loved him, and Paul Dowd supposedly loved him.

Don Dowd felt like he was the second son when Stone came along. It was all about Stone as far as his father was concerned. It didn't take long for Don to grow to resent him.

Stone loved Paul Dowd like a father and, because of the nature of their business, they spent a lot of time together. And Stone was in their home a lot. Don's mother loved Stone too. He just had a way about him. Eventually Don realized that it wasn't Stone that made his father act the way he did; that it was just his father's way. He quit feeling such anger toward Stone. It would take a number of years before the whole truth would come out; but Don started understanding the selfish motives of his dad after the drugging business. That helped him understand that Stone wasn't even a part of what drove his father.

When KingFlint and Stone were to ride in the Wood Memorial at Aqueduct in New York, Don went along with his dad for the race. He didn't mind that Paul treated him as if he was the hired hand and Stone was the son, at least it gave him a chance to be with his dad and make sure that everything went well. He was determined that KingFlint would never be drugged.

Stone was a big rider then; he had been riding for several years, had his own life, and even though he was still Paul Dowd's go-to rider, the Dowd stable was not his only big boss anymore. As happens with all of the top jockeys, every trainer wanted Stone riding for them.

But KingFlint was Stone's favorite horse. He would have ridden him if he had to ride him with two broken legs. He flew to New York from Florida the day before the race. He told Paul that Angie was coming with him and they were going to stay in New York for a couple extra days and get some rest. He had been all over the country and was just worn out.

At the last minute, Angie changed her mind. She had some school related workshop to go to and Stone came alone.

It was nasty in New York that day. It was rainy and the track was listed as sloppy which meant that there was standing water everywhere and the footing was slippery. No one was concerned; KingFlint loved the slop.

No one saw Stone until he came to the paddock. Don thought he looked tired, but he was talkative and started joking around with Paul and some of the other jockeys. No one had to give Stone instructions on KingFlint. He was the expert. Stone walked over to the horse and KingFlint put his head down on Stone's hand and then shook his head as if to say, "Come on boss, let's get to work."

One of the television personalities in the paddock stopped to ask Paul about KingFlint's chances in the Derby. Paul laughed and said that KingFlint was the one he should ask.

Several horses scratched because of the weather and there were no speed horses left in the race. Stone told Paul that he thought he would still let KingFlint lay off the lead just a little until he decided if anyone was going to run early.

As they lined up in the gate, the track announcer called all the names of the six horses and then the bell rang, the gates opened, and all six came out in a row.

Flint didn't really want the lead and Stone didn't

force him. One of the horses that normally closed took the lead and Stone could see the jockey fighting with the horse all the way around the backstretch. The horse ran well for about an eighth of a mile and then stopped dead on the track refusing to run another step.

Stone slumped over the neck of KingFlint and they took off running and won the race by about five lengths.

As KingFlint walked into the winner's circle, Paul Dowd knew something was terribly wrong. He knew it when Stone leaned over the horse's neck making it look like he was trying to get more speed out of a horse that didn't need to be making a move yet. He hoped it was some new maneuver. Paul knew Stone would never lay on the horse's neck unless he was trying to get more run from him. He and Don stared as KingFlint came toward the winner's circle.

The groom grabbed KingFlint's reins, and leaned over to pick up Stone's whip, which fell just as Stone and KingFlint got to the fence. As the groom led KingFlint in to the winner's circle area, Paul yelled at Stone. "Stone, Stone, are you okay?"

Stone was dead.

They caught him as he fell from the horse. The win was declared official, out of respect, and none of the other jockeys, trainers, or owners complained. You could have heard a pin drop in the huge Aqueduct Racetrack. Everyone stood as still as pillars, waiting and watching as the paramedics tried CPR and worked fervently on Stone. They loaded Stone onto a stretcher and put him in the ambulance and roared off to the hospital.

As they loaded him in the ambulance, the paramedic told Paul and Don that he was going in as DOA. "He has been dead for several minutes," the paramedic told Paul. "There was nothing we could do."

Word spread through the park like wildfire. "Stone Hardaway died on the track." Paul was hysterical. Don tried everything he could to comfort his dad, but he was inconsolable. Even the horse became unruly. KingFlint was very calm for a stallion, but he went crazy. He tried to kick everyone around him, and there was no one to handle him except Don. He walked the horse back to the barn and talked to him all the way.

Don was shaking. He was a young man at the time and this was something he had never encountered. Seeing his father and the people around him so shook up was more than he could deal with. And he hoped against hope that this had nothing to do with his father. He called Karen from the barn and told her the news. And then he went back to his father.

They went to the hospital and got the news from the emergency room doctor that Stone had died from an aneurysm. Don was sickened by Stone's death, but relieved it was something natural like an aneurysm. Nothing would bring Stone back, but his father could operate with a clean slate now. He knew Angie wouldn't cause them trouble; Stone died from natural causes.

Later, after the coroner had time to make his report, he told Paul that there was no way Stone could have not died instantly. He insisted that he was dead as he rode KingFlint to victory.

But they had seen him ride the race, and they had seen him ride KingFlint out after he crossed the finish line. At least they thought they had seen it. And he got KingFlint safely back to the winner's circle. They just knew he couldn't have been dead then. Paul Dowd had only one explanation for it. Stone was not going to let KingFlint lose the race. He needed the race to give him momentum for the Derby. Even if Stone knew he was dead or dying, he loved this horse and he wasn't going to let him lose his shot at the big race. It gave them all a new respect for Stone.

Paul Dowd had the unpleasant duty of calling Angie and telling her that he was gone. He hoped that she hadn't seen it on the news. The wire services picked it up and he was sure that it was on every newscast by now. Not every jockey would have made the headlines, but this wasn't just any jockey, this was "The Stone." Don remembered the sound of his father's voice that night.

He called Angie from the hotel room and Don stayed with him for moral support. He didn't envy his father's job, and he admired him very much for the way he handled the call. He hoped Angie wouldn't say anything, he had never let on to Paul that she was the one who had caused him to blow the whistle and make him stop using the performance enhancing drugs on the horses.

There was no way to make it easy on Angie. She had not accompanied Stone on the trip and everyone knew she would always regret that decision.

EIGHT

Karen remembered how painful those days were for her husband. He slowly built the farm and breeding business. Now that Don had horses that he both bred and trained, she hoped that, in time, he would be able to overcome those ghosts that had haunted him for so long. Not the ghost of Stone Hardaway, but the ghost of inadequacy, which he fought over and over.

Don never let her know that the ghosts he fought were the dark secrets he knew about Paul. She knew that Paul would never be the same. After Stone died, he hired that Central American jockey to ride KingFlint, and the horse had sustained an injury that although not life threatening, ended his racing career. The bad news was that he would never race again. The good news was that it made his price tag cheaper. With the loan, she and Don were able to buy him.

Paul Dowd retired and had never been back to the races.

Paul and Helen Dowd owned a small home in South Florida and, as far as Karen knew, Don did not see his father or mother at all anymore. She never quite understood the family relationship, but she didn't question Don about it.

When Don came home from Florida full of news about races and horses, and a new kid on the block, Karen could see the renewed energy and excitement in her husband.

So she was thankful to Bobby Tolliver for coming along, and she was thrilled that he and his little bride were such nice kids, and they were coming to Kentucky. If this gave her husband something to be excited about, then she was determined to love them.

Karen couldn't get over how young they were though. She later confided to Don that they looked like a couple of little kids. Don laughed, "They *are* a couple of little kids."

Then he told her about Bobby and Stone.

Karen was shocked that Don was talking about it as if it was an everyday occurrence. At first, she thought that he probably didn't believe it, but he talked about all the things that Stone had been teaching Bobby and she wondered if he really did believe that Stone was here. This was very much out of character for her tough, no-nonsense husband. Karen decided she would wait and see what happened. She was not one to make rash decisions. But it scared her to think about it. So, when the kids rolled into the Dowd's Kentucky farm, Karen knew everything. And although she wasn't quite sure what to expect, she was thrilled to see that they were just a couple of normal teenagers. And she was happy to take them under her wing, these two children far away from their homes and families.

The Dowd's sent the kids to stay in the little guest-house. It was not much more than a bungalow, but it had charm and was away from the big house. At last, Bobby and Sandy felt like they were really on their own.

Bobby had not decided where they were going to live yet, but he had an idea in his mind, and the place wasn't too far from here or from Lexington. He thought that he and Sandy would ride out and take a look at it.

They slept in each other's arms their first night in Kentucky and as they started to drift off to sleep, Bobby said, "Let's ride over to the old home place tomorrow. I can't wait for you to see it."

Sandy, drowsy with love and sleep said, "And I can't wait to see it."

As Bobby slipped into slumber, he dreamed of pulling into the driveway at Highway 371 and Old Hopsend Road with his bride, coming home.

It took a while to get away from the Dowd's; Don wanted to talk training and work. It was Karen who came to the rescue.

"Don, chill out, they have to get their bearings a little. There will be plenty of time for work, they need a home."

Don laughed and said he was just dying to get started on FlintRemembered's training, but for them to take their time and get settled.

As they drove away, Karen thought to herself, *They are just what the doctor ordered for all of us*. And to Don she said, "They are adorable."

He nodded his agreement.

As the kids drove through the barn area back towards the highway, Bobby spotted Stone standing at the fence, and a horse was hanging his head over the fence, eating out of his hand.

Bobby stopped the car and told Sandy he would be right back. She wondered what would cause him to stop, he was so anxious to get to the farm. But then she spotted the beautiful horse and she thought it must be one of the horses they had brought back from Florida.

He walked over to the fence and Stone smiled at him, "Hey kid, how ya doing?"

"Man, am I glad to see you! Who you got here?" Bobby asked him.

"Bobby Tolliver, I would like to introduce you to KingFlint."

Bobby shook his head. "This is KingFlint?"

Stone said, "As soon as I walked up here, he came running over. Told you he was the smartest horse I ever knew."

It was obvious that this horse did indeed know Stone, and did indeed love him. The horse nuzzled him, shook his head, then pranced and pawed the ground.

"He wants me to get on and go for a ride," Stone

said. "That's how he always acted when he wanted to run. Maybe later, boy. I am definitely gonna find a way to take you for a ride again."

Stone looked out at the car. "Where you guys headed?"

"Going over to see the home place, want to go with us?"

"You won't be able to talk to me," Stone said. "I think Sandy gets scared that you have flipped your cowboy hat when you do."

"I told you she saw you at the reception, maybe she can see you again. And she knows you are around, so it's better to just be open about it."

"I'll go, but don't make her nervous. I will be as quiet as a mouse."

Stone was anything but quiet on the ride. He was so excited about seeing KingFlint and he couldn't wait to see the two-year-old who was over at the training center. He kept raving about how good KingFlint looked and how he could step back on the track and run today.

Sandy tried to talk to Bobby but he was very distracted.

"Bobby, are you okay?" she asked finally.

"Sure baby, I am fine, why?"

"You seem so far away, and you keep nodding like you have another conversation going on in your head."

"Stone is in the car."

Sandy turned around and stared at the empty backseat.

"Why can't I see him now?"

"I don't know honey, maybe it had to do with Angie that night. I just don't know."

She frowned but said, "Hello Stone."

"Stone says hello and howdy do," Stone laughed.

Bobby grinned at her, "He's a real clown today. He says hello and howdy do."

Sandy didn't have much else to say the rest of the way until they pulled in the driveway of the farm where Bobby grew up.

"Oh my," Bobby said. "Things have gone to pot here." The place was run-down. There weren't any horses in the barns or in the field. At least ten cats were running around. The barn was in shambles, there were pieces of wood lying in piles where someone had torn down a shed and never carried away the trash.

When they pulled up to the house, a young man about the same age as Bobby came out on the porch. His face looked as if it were frozen in a perpetual scowl.

Bobby parked and stepped from the car. "Hello, is Max Stanley here?"

"Yeah," the kid said. "Who wants to know?"

"Bobby Tolliver, Colonel Robert Tolliver's grandson. We used to live here."

"Yeah, I know who you are, come on in."

Stone said, "Well if he knew who you are why did he have to ask?"

Bobby laughed. And he thought the kid looked very familiar.

A big German shepherd came running over to

them, barking at first and then cowing down and sort of half-crawling over to Stone.

"Hey boy," Stone said and leaned over and rubbed the dog's head.

"Come here, Danny," the kid called to the dog.

But he wouldn't leave Stone and followed him to the house.

"What's wrong with you, you stupid mutt?" the kid snarled at the dog.

He reached over, grabbed his collar, and tried to jerk him away. As he pulled the dog to the edge of the porch, Stone stuck out his foot, and he stumbled and almost fell.

"What the heck?" he asked and stared at Bobby.

Bobby just looked at him and said nothing. It was Sandy who said, "A lot of loose boards on this porch, someone could get hurt."

The young man tied the dog to the railing with a long rope and started back up the porch. Bobby and Sandy glanced at each other as he walked with a distinctive limp.

Stone said, "Stupid jerk, that's a great dog. See if they will throw the dog in when you buy this place."

Bobby mumbled, "Yeah right." Sandy just looked at him and shook her head.

Max Stanley was in a wheelchair and had an oxygen bottle beside him. He seemed genuinely thrilled to see Bobby.

"Emphysema, Bobby. Never take up smoking," he said, explaining the poor health. "This is my nephew

Matt Stanley, Bobby, do you remember him? Bill Hanks and he have been running the place since I got sick."

Stone said, "Yeah, running it down."

"I thought you looked familiar, Matt." Bobby stuck out his hand to shake, but the kid turned away as the old man started having a coughing fit. "What happened to all the horses Mr. Stanley? What has happened to this place?"

"I'm broke, Bobby, I lost everything in the stock market and all I had was this place. Have you come back to buy me out like you said you would?" And he had another terrible spell of coughing.

"We came to see how things were going. This is my wife, Sandy, and," he almost introduced Stone. "And I wanted her to see where I grew up."

"What are you doing now, Bobby?"

"I am about to start riding. I have been working with Don Dowd, and just got my jockey license. I plan to be at Keeneland Racetrack when they open."

"Well, how about that, we all knew you would probably be a jockey one day. Bobby, I wasn't kidding about buying me out. I am about to go to a nursing home. I can't take care of this place and I just owe a little dab on it. Matt can't take care of it, you know, he got hurt way back when and he can't do much. Bill's the only one who has stayed with me. I know it needs a lot of work, it was just too much for one man to do alone."

Bobby thought it didn't look like Bill or anyone had done anything at all since they had been gone.

How could things have gone down so much in a lit-

tle under a year and a half? he wondered. And then he thought things were probably getting bad before they left, he was just so in love with the place that he couldn't see.

"What happened to Tom Cross?" Bobby asked.

"He lives in town, moved in with his daughter after you guys left. He just sits and watches TV all day from what I hear."

"And the other guys? Marco, Pete, and Donny-O?"

"They are around, took jobs at other farms. I couldn't keep them on."

Sandy shuffled her feet and Max said, "Sorry ma'am, please have a seat." And he pointed to the couch.

"Actually, I was wondering if I could take a look around the house?"

"Well sure you can, just take off and make yourself at home."

Bobby said, "I think we will do that, and outside too, then we'll come right back and talk to you."

Max nodded and went into another fit of coughing. Matt helped him as best he could and finally got him settled down.

Sandy walked silently around the house. She looked in every room, the kitchen, and the closets. She went out on the back porch and took in the view of the pastures. Bobby walked along with her and pointed out things.

Matt came up to them in the kitchen and said sullenly, "Uncle Max said to tell you that he put all of the things you and your mother left here in the old bunkhouse. Most all of your furniture and pictures and the rest of your junk are still there. He only used one bed, and I have always slept on a cot in his room so I could take care of him."

Bobby clapped his hands. "I had forgotten that we sold this place as it was—furniture and all! We had no need of anything at Iris' house so we left it."

Sandy thought that Matt was a jerk, and she didn't smile at him even though he kept leering at her. And she couldn't understand Bobby just ignoring his "junk" remark and going on as if everything was fine.

Stone was walking from the back of the house into the kitchen and he said, "This place has distinct possibilities, but you have at least a year's worth of work to do before you can put any horses in here."

Bobby nodded and said, "We won't have the money for horses for a couple years anyway."

Sandy glared at him. And Stone could tell that it wasn't just Bobby talking to him that was making her upset.

He looked down at the floor and asked her, "What do you think?"

She reached over and took his hands, "I don't know what Stone said, but I think we can live here and work on this place ourselves. A little at a time. But I hope we don't have to see that creepy Matt guy anymore."

Bobby laughed and said, "He's harmless, just being a jerk because I got the prettiest wife in Kentucky."

They walked hand in hand back to Max and Matt.

Bobby said he would need all the financial information and he would see if the bank would even talk to him about financing.

Max was elated that they were going to try. Matt walked out to the porch out of Max's earshot and said, "Well, hotshot, you came back to be the conquering hero didn't you?"

"What are you talking about, Matt?"

"Even when we were little kids and I came over while Uncle Max visited your old granddad you were the hot shot. I remember you calling me a sissy when I fell off that pony."

"I called you a sissy because you cried like a girl and tried to hit my horse!"

"Well, you may be able to buy the place but you won't ever..." Max started yelling for Matt, who glared at Bobby, then turned to Sandy and blew her a kiss. With an evil laugh and a wink, he went back inside.

Bobby glared after him. He wanted to smash his face in, but he knew that wouldn't accomplish anything. They would see if they could actually buy the place and he would be gone and that would be the end of that.

Stone had said nothing until they climbed in the car and he said in a whisper to Bobby, even though Sandy couldn't hear him anyway, "That one is gonna be trouble, kid."

Bobby shook his head. "He will be out of our hair as soon as we buy the place and get old Max moved out."

Sandy said, "He gives me the creeps. Pretty sad when even your own dog doesn't like you."

Stone laughed and then Bobby laughed too and they began talking about the possibilities that the old farm held for them. But Stone told Bobby that he would be smart to get a mean dog, he had a bad feeling about Matt Stanley.

. . .

On the way to the Dowd's Sandy said, "If we put $30,000 in their bank, I bet they will be more inclined to talk to us, and then we can use whatever part of that we need to as a down payment."

They chatted happily as they continued to drive, with Stone chiming in about the barns and the pastures. Sandy was so happy that she didn't even mind that Bobby would answer Stone and tell her what he had said. By the time they reached Karen and Don Dowd's back drive, it was as if they had reached a place where they could co- exist without Sandy feeling left out. She even had some things to say about the farm and asked Bobby what Stone thought of her ideas.

It made Bobby very happy.

Stone seemed distracted even though he was excited about the farm. When Bobby questioned him, he said, "There is something about that Matt character that makes me nervous. I sure hope he isn't planning to stick around."

"I wouldn't think so, he's just a blowhard."

"Maybe so," Stone replied. "But I would get someone to make sure he isn't lurking around anywhere when you are gone and Sandy is there alone."

That gave Bobby the creeps and he made a mental note to see if they could keep that big dog, and to get another one if they couldn't.

He said nothing about Stone's worries to Sandy. She was very animated as she told the Dowd's about the farm. Don and Karen swore they would come and help them. Don Dowd pulled Bobby aside and told him that if he had any trouble with the bank, he would help.

Stone was thrilled for Bobby and Sandy, but he was anxious to get back to work and start training that KingFlint colt.

Bobby called Max from the bungalow and made arrangements to meet him and the banker at the house the next afternoon, all the while hoping that Matt wouldn't be there.

Sandy and Bobby deposited their money in the bank and as Sandy had hoped, the banker was more amiable than if the kids had just walked in off the street. Don Dowd wrote the bank a letter about Bobby's income and it looked as if their first home was about to become a reality.

Max Stanley was as happy as if it were his own kids buying the house. He paid the movers to come clean out the small amount of personal things he had and while they were there, they moved all of the original furnishings back into the house.

Matt was there but played the perfect helper to Uncle Max and never said another word to any of them. But just his presence gave Sandy a sick feeling in her stomach. She could feel him glare at them every time they turned their backs.

Stone wondered what it was that had him so riled up, and he watched every move the guy made. But moving day was over and Max was in a retirement home, and the last they heard was Matt was going back to Boston with his mother. Danny, the dog came to live with them, and life on the old home place began anew for Bobby Tolliver.

Sandy and Karen spent days cleaning everything from top to bottom. They bought a new refrigerator and managed to salvage the stove, but Karen insisted that Sandy have a dishwasher and she bought her one as a housewarming present.

When the dark drapes were removed there were the most beautiful bay windows in the front room; and the natural light sent sunbeams dancing across the polished hardwood floor.

Weekends were spent painting, working in the yard, and mending fences.

Stone helped Bobby when he could, always avoiding situations where other people could come in when he was there.

One afternoon while Bobby was at the Dowd's farm, Sandy looked outside and saw Matt Stanley standing at the gate to the front yard. Danny, the German shepherd started barking at him, and he flicked a cigarette in the driveway and started to walk away. He stopped at the gate and watched her as she tried to be inconspicuous as she peeked from behind the curtains. He lit another cigarette and then began limping off to the side of the road where she could see he had a truck parked.

The dog wouldn't allow Sandy to go near the door to make sure it was locked; he kept backing into her, pushing her away from the door. She felt a little better when she realized that Danny was protecting her. After she was sure that Matt had driven away, she made sure the front door was locked. Sandy told Bobby about his visit when he came home and he told her that she should always keep the doors locked when he wasn't there. But it worried him that Matt hadn't stayed in Boston, if he had really even left.

She tried to play it off as if she wasn't worried, and that she felt safe with Danny there. Bobby fixed his dog a bowl of food and as he bent over to lay the bowl on he floor, he whispered to Danny, "You are a good dog, keep a close eye on her for me, boy!"

Danny seemed to understand; he looked at Bobby with knowing eyes and then leaned over and ate his dinner.

Time flew by, the days turned into weeks and Bobby was working with the horses during the day and working at home at night.

They had the place very livable, but there was still a lot to do on the outside. Most of the work would have to wait until they had more time and some help around the place.

NINE

When the Keeneland Meet opened for its short run, Don Dowd surprised Bobby with his first ride. He was to ride in the second race of opening day in a mid-level allowance race on a three-year-old filly named NeverTardy.

As he dressed in the jockey's room, he over heard a couple of the jocks talking about him.

"Hey bug rider," one of them said. "I hear you can talk to the dead?"

Stone sat in a recliner reading the Racing Form and had been telling Bobby about the competition in the race. Stone made a face when the jockey called Bobby a bug rider. That was another name for an apprentice rider, and it wasn't bad to be called that at all, it was just that the jockey made it sound like a dirty word when he said it to Bobby.

When the jockey started in on Bobby, Stone put the Form down and listened.

Bobby ignored him and continued dressing.

"Hey you, bug boy, didn't you hear what I asked you?"

Bobby turned around slowly and said, "What was your stupid question?"

Several of the other jockeys laughed.

"I hear you talk to a dead jockey."

"You don't look dead to me," Bobby said and the room erupted in laughter.

Stone smiled and picked up the paper and continued reading.

Bobby adjusted his tie, took one last look in the mirror, and left the jockey's room.

As they walked to the paddock, the belligerent jockey said to him under his breath, "Stay out of my way on the track!"

"I don't think that will be a problem, Carlos. The horse you are riding will be so far back that we will look like a speck on the horizon. We won't be in your way—we will just be out of the way...way ahead."

Bobby walked over to where Don was standing with Terry Fulton, the owner of NeverTardy.

Terry Fulton was a very wealthy man, with a large string of horses. Don Dowd had wanted to be his trainer for a long time and Fulton had finally given him four of his horses. NeverTardy was the first of them to race.

As Bobby walked up, he overheard Terry Fulton telling Don that he couldn't believe that Don was putting a snot-nosed bug on one of his best fillies.

Bobby ignored him, and shook his hand when Don introduced them.

Fulton said, "Kid, you better win this race."

Don Dowd told Fulton that he trusted Bobby completely.

The race was anything but uneventful.

As they waited in the gate for the other horses to load, Bobby could feel his heart pounding. The horse was quiet and well behaved in the gate, and Bobby hoped she couldn't tell that he was nervous. A confident jockey makes a confident horse.

Bobby's horse was a speed horse and there was one other speed horse in the race. But NeverTardy was very relaxed as she left the gate so Bobby let the other horse set blistering fractions and he and NeverTardy lay just off the lead about two lengths behind.

As they made the first turn in the mile and sixteenth race, another horse attempted to get in position for a run. Unfortunately, she wanted the very spot on the track that NeverTardy had.

The horse bumped her and just as Bobby was about to try to move her to the outside away from trouble, Carlos took his stick and slapped NeverTardy across the face and then swung the stick again and slapped Bobby across the hand causing him to drop his whip. Bobby hadn't noticed until then that it was Carlos riding the horse.

"I told you to stay out of my way, ghost boy," and

he took another swing at Bobby. NeverTardy seemed to sense that this was not a friendly encounter and when Bobby clicked and whistled, she kicked into another gear and took off. As hard as he tried, Carlos' horse was not able to catch up to NeverTardy.

She easily won the race by several lengths.

When Bobby returned with her to the winner's circle, Terry Fulton was screaming at the trainer of the horse that had compromised NeverTardy. He and Don filed an objection, the stewards posted the Inquiry sign, and after a few minutes, they disqualified the horse Carlos was riding from fourth to last place.

Stone was yelling at the jockey as he walked by and Bobby had to yell at Stone to keep him from slugging him.

Sandy came to the winner's circle and had her picture made with Bobby and the rest of the connections of the horse. She smiled, thoroughly excited. But she had questions about the incident on the track.

"Why did that guy do that, Bobby?" she asked.

"Just being a jerk, honey. I am okay. That's what matters. Don't worry."

Stone stood nearby and he said, "He could have gotten you killed out there! That's not fun and games. That was a very intelligent little filly you were on, she could have really gone nuts on you!"

"She is a great little horse," Bobby said calmly, and then he yelled. "I won my first race, I won my first race!" And he hugged Sandy, did a high five with Stone, and danced around for a minute celebrating.

Then like a kid, he clapped and danced all the way

back to the jockey's room to take off the silks of Terry Fulton and dress in the silks of Don Dowd for the next race he was scheduled to ride.

Sandy went back to the stands and sat down. Stone came over and sat down beside her.

I like this girl. She is a good woman for her jockey husband, as her Aunt would have been, he thought.

Stone stared out at the track and thought about Angie and some of the races she had watched just like this one. He figured she had watched many of them with her heart in her throat. He'd had some harrowing times on the track.

. . .

Stone wondered if Angie ever wished she had fallen in love with a banker instead of a jockey. If she ever thought it, he never knew. She adored him and he never doubted it for a minute.

Stone and Angie met at the supermarket. That was always their private joke. They never told another soul where they met, or how.

Stone was picking out a few groceries in the produce section. Angie was shopping nearby.

A woman was shopping with her toddler child. The mother walked over two aisles to get something off the shelf and left the kid alone in the basket. The kid was crying to get out and when he stood up he tried to climb out of the basket and in the process, he slipped and fell.

Stone hadn't been paying any attention to anyone in the store, but he heard the crying child and looked up just in time to see him. Stone dropped his lettuce and dived toward the basket. He caught the child as he fell. Both of them ended up on the floor in a heap, with Stone on the bottom, and the child, unhurt but scared to death, on top of him.

The mother ran over and started screaming at Stone. She thought he was trying to take her kid! It made Angie so angry that she got right up in the mother's face and was telling her what a sorry parent she was when the store manager and a security person separated them.

Stone stood off to the side and watched as this pretty lady jumped to his defense and stood toe to toe, all four feet, ten of her, with this enraged mother who towered over her. The manager was able to get everyone calmed down and after he heard Angie's story and talked to Stone, he felt confident that the mother was the one at fault for leaving her child unattended in the basket.

He offered his sincerest thanks to Stone for saving the baby from a bad fall, insisted the mother thank him also, and then spoke very kindly to Angie. She was still livid, but he congratulated her on being so observant and able to tell them what had happened.

The mother left with her baby still crying with confusion. Angie looked rather embarrassed about throwing such a fit when the mother was accusing Stone of trying to take her baby. She didn't even know this guy and she ran to his defense as if she was Joan of Arc. Now she was red-faced and wanted to get out of there as soon as she could. She made a mental note to herself not to ever shop here again.

Stone finally was able to laugh about it and he told Angie that he owed her nothing less than dinner for being his "Lady in Shining Armor."

She tried to beg off, but after she spent a few minutes with Stone, she didn't put up too much of a fight. She found him charming and sweet.

They had dinner that night at a nice restaurant in Fort Lauderdale, across the street from the beach, and after dinner, they took a walk.

Angie Wagner was not just beautiful; she was intelligent and witty. Stone laughed at her jokes and they had a wonderful time. He hated to hear the words, "Well, I had better be going."

Angie was in her second year of teaching. Stone was in his fourth year of riding. They had nothing in common. Angie had never been to the track, so Stone invited her out for the races the following Saturday.

He was riding for Paul Dowd among others and figured he would have a trip or two to the winner's circle. He thought she might get a kick out of being there with the connections and having her picture made with him and the horse.

She came out to Gulfstream Park and sat in the dining room with Paul Dowd's wife Helen.

When he won his first race, he looked for her, and as she had promised, Helen Dowd brought Angie to the winner's circle and handed her over to Stone. She was even more beautiful than he remembered.

Stone could still see her with her shy smile that day. She wasn't sure what to do, and the photographer embarrassed her when he said, "Step over by your husband, Mrs. Hardaway. We want to be sure we get you in this picture."

Stone couldn't stop smiling. He thought she had such a beautiful name and Hardaway seemed to be a perfect last name to go with it.

It was quite a while before they got around to talking about marriage. And by the time they did, it wasn't such a big deal to either of them.

Now Stone wished he had done what Bobby and Sandy did and just insisted they elope and never look back.

Angie asked Stone one time if it would make him happy to be married. He told her that he already felt married to her, that a piece of paper was just a piece of paper. She said it was proof of their commitment to each other; he said he was committed to her already.

Now as he thought back about it, he could see the signals she was sending. But he was a dope and thought that because she didn't just come out and say she wanted them to get married that she was okay with the way things were. He would have married her on the spot, all she had to do was say so.

Later when they talked about having kids, Stone would have nothing but marriage before they tried. They bought a house together, and when he wasn't on the road, they worked in the yard. They put in a pool and a hot tub and they made the place their own little bit of paradise.

When Stone was on the road, he yearned for Angie and home. His most happy days were when they were home, just the two of them.

Stone came from a large family of all boys. His father was a coal miner, and he had no other ambition for his sons than they follow in his footsteps and go to work in the mines as soon as they were old enough.

Stone wasn't of a mind to die of black lung. He didn't want to spend his days in darkness. He could not see climbing in and out of a filthy black hole in the earth coated in soot from head to toe.

His mother was a sweet woman who suffered with the burden of taking care of a belligerent miner and his drunken Saturday nights and dropping a kid every year.

When Stone refused to go to see the foreman about a job when he turned sixteen, his father threw him out. His mother cried and begged his father to relent and let Stone stay and try to get a job somewhere other than the mines, but his father blew up and accused her of making him a sissy.

Stone didn't want any more grief for his mother so he packed his two shirts, his one pair of long pants, some underwear and started hitchhiking, not sure, where he was headed.

Stone was a small-boned guy. He had height, he was about 5'6," but he was thin. Very thin. Weight had never been a problem for him. He had a high rate of metabolism and he could eat all he cared to and never gain a pound.

One of the people who picked him as he hitchhiked

was a guy named Keith Beck. Keith Beck was a trainer. A horse trainer. He had a nice stable of horses. He talked Stone into coming along with him to Florida, offered him a job as a hot walker, and started training him to ride.

Stone was a natural. The kid had never even seen a horse except in books and here he was riding them.

He learned a lot from Keith Beck. But he wasn't going to get to stay with him long; Keith got into trouble with the Internal Revenue Service and they took everything they could from him. He folded up what he had left and moved back to Connecticut. But he did Stone Hardaway a great favor and introduced him to Paul Dowd, telling Paul that Stone was one of his best men. And he did Paul a favor by introducing him to Stone. And as they say, the rest is history.

Stone went back to West Virginia to see his parents one time after he began his riding career. His father told him to get out and never come back. So Stone obliged, and never went back. Stone frequently sent his mother money, or he did until the last letter was returned saying that addressee was deceased. After that, he never tried contacting any of them again.

But he always wondered about his brothers. He was pretty sure they were all at the bottom of a coal mine.

Angie asked about his family and after he told her about them, she never mentioned it again. She knew Stone well enough that if he felt the need to go see them, or talk about them, he would. She was his best friend. She was the love of his life . She was his confidant. They shared everything, and obviously, he felt no obligation to the family he left behind.

But she could tell that it was very important for him to have a family of his own. But for whatever reason, it was sufficient for them to just have each other for the time being. She would know when he was ready to have children.

Stone smiled as he thought about the conversation they had about babies the first time. He joked with Angie that he really didn't care for kids. She, being a schoolteacher, loved them and wished for a house full. He told her that he came from a family with a house full and that had been plenty for him.

He carried the joke on for a long time before he could tell that she was about ready to cry and he had to hold her and kiss her to get her over being mad at him. He never joked about kids again.

TEN

Sandy stirred beside Stone and he came out of his reverie and heard her yelling for Bobby. He was on another horse, this one for Don Dowd and he had just taken the lead.

The horse won the race without any incidents on the track, and Stone saw Sandy breathe a big sigh of relief.

He wondered if the name calling by the other jockeys was going to bother Bobby. He was such a good kid, and he was so even tempered that Stone doubted they would be able to get him upset. But, it had to be distracting. And the last thing a jockey needs when he is riding is distractions.

Stone reminded himself to tell Bobby how to fall the next time they had a chance to have a training session. He had seen too many of his friends end up injured and out for weeks or crippled for life. This was not the easiest nor safest sport in the world. He just wanted the kid to be healthy a long time.

Stone watched Sandy go join her husband once again in the winner's circle. Stone expected Bobby to spend a lot of time there.

The days he was riding in races around the country, Sandy stayed home to get some work done.

And she began to plan something that would be a great surprise for him.

Danny turned out to be great company for her as well as making her feel safer. And, she could always tell when Stone was around by the way the dog reacted.

It seemed like all the animals loved Stone, even this dog.

Bobby had become an overnight sensation. He was getting riding offers from all over the country. He was winning 38% of his races and was in the money almost 100% of the time. He was a trainer and owner's dream.

But he stayed busy with Don and Stone, working with FlintRemembered. The moment he laid eyes on that two-year old—when it stepped off the trailer ramp and turned around—it was love at first sight.

Stone fell just as head over heels for him as Bobby did.

"He is KingFlint made over," Stone said. "Look at him, right down to the blaze on his face."

And the horse was a dream to work with. He had the most beautiful gait and such a pleasant demeanor. Bobby would rather be at the farm working with FR as they affectionately began to call him, than on the racetrack riding for money. Almost.

He was having so much fun, and Sandy was so happy watching him live his dream. Their parents came up several times and went to the track with Sandy. Joy watched most of his races with one eye covered and her heart racing in her chest.

Word had gotten around everywhere that Bobby talked to "the ghost jockey." And he took a lot of flak, some good natured, some nasty, from the other jockeys and even from some fans. But he just smiled and went on about his business of winning races and making them look small and mean-spirited.

The Racing Form called him Bobby Phenom, and he was constantly being asked for interviews. He would be ready to talk racing and they would want to talk ghosts. Bobby was usually so nice and good-natured but after one interviewer started out asking about Stone and asked Bobby to ask Stone some questions, he blew up and told the guy to call Stone's agent and set up an interview with him.

Stone began to get tired of it as well. "Why can't these idiots see you have so much talent that you don't need anything supernatural helping you? The other jocks are just jealous but I can't understand the crowds reacting the way they do."

"Hopefully it'll pass," Bobby said. "If I just ignore them, they get quiet after the second or third race. And if they have money bet on me, I am their hero, and they don't care if I talk to gophers."

Bobby started getting letters from people asking him to contact their lost loved ones.

Even Stone began to get letters from fans as well. They would address his letters "in care of" Bobby Tolliver. It was driving Sandy crazy.

But Bobby was right. After a few months, most of the teasing stopped and he was able to do his job. Ever so often, a nut would call their house or mail a letter asking Stone to contact good old Uncle Henry and ask where he had buried the loot, but Sandy and Bobby just laughed about it. Bobby even asked Stone to ask old Henry where the loot was and *he* would go get it.

After a while, things calmed down and everyone was able to just concentrate on doing their job.

FR was coming along beautifully. The plan was to race him in a stakes race for two-year-olds in Louisville. He had been training so well that Don felt confident that this was the perfect time to start him.

Bobby loved riding him, FlintRemembered trained as if he had been doing it all of his life. Bobby told Stone that he should ride FlintRemembered, but Stone told Bobby that he would rather ride KingFlint. They waited for an opportunity to come along.

. . .

And then FlintRemembered got sick.

Don was grief stricken, he told Bobby that this was his fourth KingFlint colt to get the colic. The other three had died and it was beginning to look as if the same would happen to FlintRemembered.

Stone found the fact that all of KingFlints colts had

died of colic too much of a coincidence to be ignored. Standing outside the barns, he talked to Bobby about it.

"Something is going on with this horse. He was fine when he came back from the Training Center."

"You know how colic is, Stone. It strikes these babies all of a sudden. And Don said the others had done exactly the same thing."

"I don't like it. I am going to do some snooping around." Bobby and Don paced around the barn and waited for the vet to finish examining FR.

He came from the stall shaking his head, "Sorry, Don," he said. "I don't think he is going to live out the night."

Don yelled and cussed. "Isn't there something you can do? Something new you can try?"

"I don't know what it would be," Doc said.

Stone came walking up as the three men stood talking.

"Bobby," he said. "FR is being poisoned."

Bobby looked at Stone and asked, "What would make you say that?"

The vet assumed he was talking to him and he replied, "Well, there just aren't a lot of remedies for colic that has gotten this far along."

"Just ask him about poisoning, Bobby!"

"What if FR was being poisoned?" Bobby asked.

Don and the Vet both stared at Bobby.

"Why would you ask that, Bobby?" Don asked.

"Just grasping at straws, Don."

Doc shook his head, "What could he have gotten in to that would have poisoned him?"

Stone said, "Someone has been feeding him poison."

Bobby asked the vet the question again.

"Well," the vet said. "There would be an entirely different treatment than for colic."

Don looked puzzled, "What are you getting at, Bobby? Who in the world would poison my horses?"

Stone said to Bobby, "Ask Don where he knows that Iggy from. How long has he worked for him?"

Bobby looked at Stone with his mouth open and said, "No, that can't be possible. He's a long-time employee."

The vet looked at Don and at Bobby and stared at the space where Bobby had directed his question.

"Just ask him, Bobby!" Stone yelled.

"Don, where did Iggy come from? How long has he worked for you?"

Don gasped, "Not Iggy, he has been with me since I got KingFlint. He used to work for my...oh *no*!" he yelled at the vet. "Do it, Doc, check him out for poison!" And then he took off running for the bunkhouse with Bobby and Stone right behind him.

Iggy came to the door and looked at the two men and Bobby immediately saw the fear in his eyes.

"Why Iggy? Don asked. Why would you kill my horses? He put you up to it, didn't he? The sorry old..."

"Señor Don, I am so sorry. I don want to do it, but my brother has no work, your family make him no possible to ride no more. I have to help him get the revenge."

"Your brother? Who is your brother? What would he have to do with my farm? Did he work for me?"

Iggy stared at the ground and then he said in a half whisper, "Esteban Escobar, he is my brother.

It was that horse's get, I have to make sure no more Flint horses to chase roses. For my brother, Señor Don."

"Esteban Escobar! You told me your last name was Velez. All these years I have only known you as Iggy Velez...you did this for Esteban? Why me? Why my horses? Esteban worked for my father."

Iggy looked sadly at Bobby and back at Don. "Senor Don, I feel very bad but it is family."

Don turned and started to walk away. Bobby knew it was to regain his composure. If Don felt the anger that Bobby felt at this moment he would have strangled this man with his bare hands.

Stone was livid. "Where is he going? This idiot needs to go to jail! The old man would have lynched him right here on the spot."

Bobby stood to the side and waited for Don to walk back over.

"Get your stuff and get out, Iggy. You have three hours to get out. I am calling the cops. Don't ever think about getting another job in Kentucky, or anywhere else I race my horses. You are done for!"

Iggy nodded and went inside.

"If my horse dies, I am not sure what I will do to him, but he had better be long gone!" Don walked back to the barn and Stone and Bobby followed.

"How did you know, Stone? How did you figure

it out?" Bobby asked. Why didn't you say something about your suspicions when FR went off his feed? We knew something was up."

"Bobby, you can't say anything until you have all of the facts. FR was just acting a little colicky, Iggy was poisoning him the smart way, slowly, so no one would suspect anything. At first, I even thought he was feeding him from the different feed to help him with the colic. When he took the turn for the worse, I went to the feed stall and found nothing, but when I searched Iggy's room at the bunkhouse I found the insecticide he was adding to his oats to poison him. Two and two are still four, kid. I just hope we found out in time."

Don asked Bobby what gave him the idea that Iggy was poisoning the horse. Bobby stared at Don and said, "I'm not sure you want to know the answer to that question, Don."

"Why wouldn't I?"

"Because it was Stone who solved the puzzle, not me. He just told me to ask the questions I asked."

Don was silent for a full minute and then he said, "Tell Stone I said thanks."

Bobby smiled, "You just did."

When Don told Karen about Iggy and the poison, she cried. "We should have had the other colts autopsied. Remember GoldFlick? He suffered so much before he died. Poor FR, do you think he will be okay?"

And then it was all Don could do to keep Karen in the house. She was so angry that she wanted to punch Iggy. And she insisted they call the police. She told

Don and Bobby she didn't care if he went to jail for life. That this was a terrible thing to do to an animal. Don knew Karen was being irrational, but she loved the horses and anything that happened to them she took personally. While they waited for the police to come take a report, Don told her about Stone and Bobby solving the mystery and she shivered.

"You mean, Bobby thinks Stone is here?"

"Yes," Don replied.

"What do you think Don?" She asked.

"I don't know, honey. The common sense part of me says it's impossible, and the other part of me, the part that sees Bobby everyday and knows what the kid is learning from somebody, well…I just don't know. I do know that Bobby loves him, and Sandy won't admit it but she thinks he is here too, and well, even that darned KingFlint acts like he's a colt again, so something is going on. That's all I can tell you."

Karen laughed a small laugh. "Well, I guess if it makes everyone so happy to believe it, then what harm can it do?"

Don said, "None, I hope."

ELEVEN

FlintRemembered did recover but the process was a slow one. They took him by ambulance that evening to the vet's hospital and it was five days before he returned to the farm. He was weak for quite a while. Bobby and Stone took turns guarding him and pampering him after he came home.

KingFlint snorted and stomped in his stall and Stone said he knew something was going on.

The police found Iggy and took him to jail. But he was booked on a misdemeanor offense and released when someone paid the fine. The police told the Dowd's that after the animal cruelty charges anything else would be a civil matter and they could sue him. They knew that he had nothing, but they did set out to get his work permit in the U.S. revoked and have him deported, along with his brother who they found working under another name on a farm a hundred miles from theirs. A few weeks after Iggy's arrest, Don had a call from the INS and they asked him if he also went by the name Paul Dowd. When he told them he didn't and asked why, the officer told him that Paul Dowd had hired Esteben and was the brother's sponsor for work in the U.S. Don asked him how long that had been going on and was told since 1979.

Don was sick. Since four years after Stone died and he and Karen bought KingFlint, his father had these two on his payroll. That meant Paul put them up to killing off his colts.

He still said nothing to Karen. He had never kept but this one secret from her before, and now he had to keep another.

He called Paul from his cell phone.

When he heard his father's voice on the phone, his blood boiled, "Why Dad? Why would you try to hurt me like this? We could have been ruined."

There was silence on the line and then Paul Dowd said, "Paybacks are paybacks, son." And he hung up.

Don stood with the phone in his hand and stared at it. That was it? All because he had threatened to tell the authorities that he was doping his horses? For wanting to make the old man do what was right?

Paul Dowd told him years ago that he had the best rider in the world on the horses. Paul would speed them up and Stone would relax them; it was a perfect combination. Perfect except that he had caused Stone to suffer needless injuries. And he was supposed to love Stone so much. And for what? Money? Prestige? Don figured out then that his father was just a bad man, spurned on by greed, and lacking in compassion for anyone. And there is nothing you can do about a bad man, except thank your lucky stars if you find out in time to steer clear.

So he had never loved Stone, he just used him. Don felt bad about having hard feelings about Stone all these years. Stone was just like him, just another patsy in his dad's scheme to be rich and prominent.

Don put the phone in his pocket and walked back to the barn. He felt like a huge weight had just been taken off his shoulders. At last, he had come to terms with his relationship with Paul Dowd. He wasn't worth the trouble. Now, he just wished it hadn't taken so many years to figure him out.

He whistled all the way back to the barn,

The hands found it very strange to see him almost happy after all that had happened.

. . .

The poisoning incident set FR's training back several months and he missed the race at Churchill Downs so Don set a goal for The Hopeful Stakes at Saratoga in August.

After FR got well, Bobby and Don worked even harder training him. They took him by trailer to Ellis Park for a prep race before heading to New York and Saratoga. He had not even run in a maiden race yet. All he had were training races and he had won every one of them. He had gate works and bullet works; everything pointed to a superstar in the making. Now he needed a real race.

Bobby asked about Don about taking KingFlint with them to Ellis Park to let him stretch his legs. Don was surprised. He told Bobby that KingFlint was barn sour and would act like a fool if he got on the track, but Bobby pleaded with Don and he agreed. Both of the Flint's looked beautiful in their stalls side by side in the cozy confines of Ellis Park.

Don was not a fool, he had a pretty good idea why Bobby asked for KingFlint to go along. It wasn't just for the ride, he decided that it was for Stone. But when nothing unusual happened, Don decided he was just being paranoid.

Stone was itching to ride KingFlint. There were always too many people around at the farm and at the training center. Early in the morning or late in the evening would be a perfect time to ride at the racetrack. He hammered Bobby about it from the moment they arrived at Ellis Park.

"You are worse than a little kid, Stone," Bobby said with a laugh. Just hold your horses."

Stone laughed at Bobby's pun and replied, "Wow, kid. You have turned into a real Groucho Marx."

Bobby wasn't sure who that was but it didn't sound too bad so he just smiled and shook his head.

Sandy called Bobby on his cell phone and said she couldn't wait for him to come home; she had a big surprise. Bobby told her he would be home in three days, but asked her if she wanted him to make the three-hour drive over and she said that she would wait and see him when he got home. Bobby spent the next three days trying to figure out what the surprise could be.

In the late afternoon after most everyone had gone for the day, Don Dowd told Bobby that he was going to go home, but he would return the next day just before post time. Bobby decided this was the perfect opportunity, and he told Stone to saddle KingFlint.

Stone told him that he needed to ride along too or it would look like there was a loose horse on the track and someone would take notice.

Bobby saddled FR and met Stone on the track.

Don started to drive away and remembered that he had not been to the Racing Secretary's office about the race they were scheduled to run on Saturday. He wanted to get the scratch in now. He was taking the horse, UnifiedProspect, home. She had been acting as if she felt bad and she had a cough, so he wanted his own vet to take a look at her.

He parked the car, ran up the steps to the secretary's office, and found it locked. He decided he would tell Bobby and he could be there to do it first thing in the morning. As he walked from the offices to the outside grandstand area, he saw the two Flint's on the track. Don stepped back and watched from a hidden alcove. He spotted someone at the window of an upstairs office and realized Ron Geary, the President of Ellis Park, was watching. Don was relieved when he closed the blinds. He wasn't sure how he would have explained this to Ron.

KingFlint was a true thing of beauty on the racetrack. He acted as if he had just been away for a day as he pranced and tossed his head. He pulled at the bit and Stone said to Bobby as he rode alongside, "He wants to run!"

And like a choreographed ballet of muscle and manes, the two horses ran at a gallop around the track.

Don knew someone was riding KingFlint then. The horse behaved just as FlintRemembered did with his rider. He watched as the two horses bent their heads and practically danced the last eighth of a mile. Bobby had his head back laughing and talking to the formless rider on KingFlint.

Don Dowd stepped far back into the shadows before either could see him. This was a private engagement, and he didn't want to spoil it for either man. And he didn't want them to see the big, tough trainer crying like a baby.

. . .

FlintRemembered broke his maiden in the Ellis Park race. He was the only first timer entered in the Maiden Special Weight race, and he won the race with ease. Bobby knew they had a real jewel on their hands. He rode out like he could have gone another mile and a half.

As they celebrated in the winner's circle, Don said, "You remind me of something they used to say about Stone, Bobby."

"What's that?"

"His name may be Stone, but he rides as light as a feather."

"I hope I can be half the jockey he is," Bobby said

"Was," Stone reminded him.

"He had a good reputation didn't he?" Bobby asked Don, while casting a smile at Stone.

"Oh yes, he was well respected, but a lot of people resented him because he always found a way to win. 'He wins one way or the Hardaway,' they would say. But people liked him, some were jealous of him, but he was such a good guy that they couldn't help but like him. I never really knew him that well, he and my dad were really close though. I did know one thing about him, Bobby—he was one great jockey."

Bobby smiled at Stone and said, "Well, he thinks he was anyway, and we won't say anything different, we don't want to make him feel bad."

Stone laughed, " You are really funny, ghost boy!" And they both laughed.

Don just shook his head and wished he could have heard both sides of the conversation.

. . .

It was getting late in the afternoon when Bobby drove up in his driveway. He was tired and ready to be home. He felt like he had been away from Sandy for months instead of only a few days.

As soon as he put the car in park, she came flying out the front door. He opened the car door, grabbed her, swung her around, and kissed her.

"Now this, he said with a smile, is the kind of surprise I like!"

"Silly, this is not your surprise. Come in the house and I will tell you what it is."

She carried one of his bags and they entered the house holding hands.

Everything was sparkling clean. He had to admit that Sandy was a wonderful housekeeper and cook, and something smelled delicious.

He looked at the table and it was set for three.

With a disappointed look he asked, "Who is joining us?"

And from the corner of the living room a voice said, "Well, I guess that would be me."

And he looked over and saw Tom Cross.

"Oh my gosh, Tom, is that you?" And he ran over and grabbed the old man.

Tom pulled back with his hands on Bobby's arms and said, "Well look at the Tolliver kid now would ya? Not a kid anymore."

Bobby turned to Sandy and she stood there beaming at the two men.

"This, Bobby said to her, is a wonderful surprise."

"Tom is coming to work for us, Bobby. He's going to be foreman."

"Well, how in the world did you find him? And he turned to Tom. How did she find you?"

"Wasn't hard, he said, she just followed the sound of my whining. I have been miserable since you and Miss Joy left. Old Stanley let the place go to…oh sorry,

Miss Sandy, and I couldn't take it anymore. I would have worked here till I died with or without a paycheck, but I couldn't stand that Bill Hanks and the way he let things just fall down around him after Stanley took to the wheelchair. And that crazy nephew of his..." Tom shook his head. He was always sneaking around...made me a nervous wreck."

"Yeah, Bobby said, I was sick when we pulled in the yard and saw the place. What is it with Matt Stanley anyway?"

Tom shook his head. "You don't remember? He stole GoldenLeer, your grandfather's Derby winning stud, took him out in the pasture, the horse bolted on him, and he broke his hip and leg. They thought Matt wouldn't ever walk again, but he gimps along all right I heard."

"I only remember bits and pieces of that incident," Bobby said.

"That kid was always trying to imitate you, he was jealous I think because you were such a good rider and your grandfather just doted on you. He didn't have anyone except old Max and I honestly don't think Max could stand him."

"I thought his mother lives in Boston?"

"His mother? Tom laughed. "She's in Boston all right, locked away in a sanitarium for the mentally ill. She killed Matt's brother when he was five years old. She hanged him. They said she was going to get Matt too but he ran away. That's how come Matt to be here with Max Stanley."

Sandy shivered. "Oh poor guy."

"You never know about people, some of the old timers around here figured he was just as crazy as his momma. Has he been around here?"

Sandy said he had.

Tom said, "We need to make sure we keep a good close eye on you, Miss Sandy." And he winked at Bobby. "But this place just looks great now, you have done a wonderful job. I don't know how you got such a fine young lady as this one to put up with you." He put his arms around Sandy's shoulders.

"Oh that was easy, with all this charm and my good looks, Bobby laughed. But, until we can afford some horses, there isn't going to be much to do around here."

"Oh, don't forget your humility, Sandy added laughing. And I am sure we can find something to keep Tom busy."

They had a wonderful dinner and Tom showed Bobby what he had already done with the bunkhouse to make it livable for himself. And, in time he assured Bobby, they would have more help. Tom could see this place would be a prosperous farm once again.

As Sandy and Bobby lay in each other's arms that night, she said, "I hope you will feel good about leaving me here when you have to be on the road. I feel better now that Tom will be here."

Bobby said he hoped he wouldn't have to leave her very often, and he told her about the month of August in upstate New York.

TWELVE

Saratoga Springs is a most beautiful place. There are huge old trees and mountains in the distance. But, it turns from a quaint little village into a bustling, crowded circus town for thirty-six days in the summer. Every hotel, motel, and inn is filled to capacity with crowds from all over the country. Saratoga Springs becomes Saratoga Raceway, and everything is forgotten, except for the horse.

Bobby and Sandy stayed in a lovely hotel in Lake George, twenty-five miles from the track. Lake George was another quaint village. It was built around the crystal blue lake for which the village was named and snuggled at the foot of the Adirondack Mountains. Thomas Jefferson once called it "a beautiful jewel." Even Lake George was busy during this time of the year, and the traffic was terrible. But Sandy and Bobby didn't care. It was heaven.

There was a horseracing museum across the street from one of the main gates of the track and Bobby wanted to go in and look around.

"Stone said they would see a few pictures of him there," Bobby told Sandy.

There were more than a few pictures of Stone Hardaway.

Stone had been a summer fixture at Saratoga. He won the Traver's Stakes an unprecedented four times in his riding career, along with numerous other stakes races at the grand old track.

Sandy was interested in the pictures because in several of them, taken in the winner's circle, Angie had been there. It almost made her start crying to see her aunt's pictures and the happiness on her face.

Stone was behind them as they wandered along through the museum, and he spotted the pictures with Angie. He had forgotten about the winner's circle pictures. He hadn't remembered her being there when they took the pictures of the horses and rider. It caught him by surprise.

He had loved having her with him at the racetrack. And he loved having her with him in the winner's circle. She was so pretty, and she always stood so close to him and put her arm around his waist. He would pull her close to him after the pictures and sneak a kiss. She would look at him with those beautiful eyes and he would have to hide in the jockey's room to keep from gathering her in his arms and running away from the crowds.

She melted him. And he wasn't sure that he liked someone having such power over him. But then she would just say his name and he would look at her, and she would look at him with such love that he didn't care if the entire world knew he was a powerless wimp in her presence.

The pictures on the wall of the museum stabbed Stone like a knife in his heart. He stayed long enough to get a heart full of Angie's face and he turned and almost ran from the museum.

Bobby and Sandy walked over to another exhibit and Bobby looked around to see if Stone was still there. He saw him as he ran from the museum, and he understood perfectly how he felt.

FlintRemembered was getting a lot of press. This was a great human-interest story of the sire that almost was a Derby horse, and the colt that almost wasn't. Add the apprentice jockey Bobby Phenom and you had all the makings of a media circus.

Don Dowd spent a lot of time in interviews, which he hated. Bobby was trying to ride other races and was getting his picture taken so much—not only in the winner's circle but everywhere he and Sandy went—that it became almost impossible to leave the hotel or the jockey's room. Sandy began to wish she had stayed home. Every time she went anywhere, including the ladies restroom on the second floor clubhouse, she was bombarded with questions.

And without exception, everyone wanted to know about Stone Hardaway.

"Does Bobby still see him?" Question after question. Same questions over and over.

Stone was glad that he couldn't answer some of these stupid questions, and he felt bad for Bobby—but especially for Sandy—that they had to go through this.

Stone asked Bobby if he would rather he went back to Kentucky.

Bobby laughed, taking it all in stride and he replied, "*You* aren't the problem, it's these people who keep asking me the same stupid questions *about you* that drive us crazy."

And here in Saratoga, where the best of the best come to ride, the jockeys started to give him a hard time, which really surprised both Bobby and Stone. One guy told him that he was giving racing a bad image. Another said that he had better ask God for forgiveness for buying into that spirit crap.

Even the big name jockeys made "ghost" remarks.

Paul Daily told him that Stone Hardaway had been a friend of his and he always liked him, but that he didn't think there were such things as ghosts, and he couldn't imagine Stone as a ghost anyway.

Jerome Beal asked Bobby if Stone rode on the back of his horse, or if he just floated alongside him.

Eddie Vasquez kept saying, "Come out, Stone. Come out, Stone." And he would jump around corners and yell, Are you here, Stone?"

Stone was getting angrier and angrier with his former friends and fellow riders, but Bobby still continued to mostly ignore them.

He told Stone and Sandy that he was just going to let his riding do his talking.

And he said, "That I win is a credit to Stone and all he has taught me." It made Stone very proud.

Race day arrived rainy and cool. Three horses scratched from the race at the beginning of the day and Don actually considered scratching FR just because he was still so young and inexperienced, and had never been on an "off-track."

Bobby sort of hoped that he would. He wanted nothing to cause this horse to be injured. Especially not a wet track.

Stone told Bobby to keep his cool, he said, "King-Flint loved the slop, and FR runs from off the pace, or seems like he will be happy that way, so don't worry about getting out there and trying to set the track on fire. All these two-year-olds know how to do is to take off running as soon as the gate opens. Your horse won't want to do that if you just relax him on the backstretch, then you will have all the horse you need when you make the turn for home."

"But is he going to like having that mud thrown in his face?" Bobby asked.

"Keep him on the outside of the field, off the rail, that rail is heavy and not the place to be in the slop. He won't be that far off the pace and you should be able to make your run just as soon as you make the turn for home. Remember it's a short stretch run. And don't feel nervous or the horse will feel it. He will think you don't have confidence in him."

Bobby nodded. And everyone noticed that he was talking to no one.

As he dressed in the jockey's room, one of the jockeys said, "Hey kid, whose really gonna ride this race, you or the great Stone Hardaway?

Bobby stood quietly for a moment and then he turned and looked at him and said, "You'd better hope it's me, 'cause if Stone rides, you jerks sure won't stand a chance!" And he turned back around and put on his hat.

The race played out just as Stone had thought it would. There wasn't a lot of speed, and with the three scratches, there was only seven horses left in the field.

FlintRemembered did lay right off the lead and outside the compact field. Bobby kept him to the task and as they made the turn, he asked FR for his run and the horse responded with a great burst of speed.

They easily won the race and he hadn't really asked FR for his best.

When he told Don afterward how well the horse had behaved, Don heaved a big sigh of relief and said, "Bobby, I think we really might have our Derby horse."

They stayed another week in New York and then went home.

On the plane, Stone sat in an empty seat across the aisle from Bobby and talked to him while Sandy napped.

"There are some things I need you to think about, kid. Remember that horses hate the gate, it's like walking into a coffin for them. I noticed that FR still doesn't feel good in the gate, he seemed very uneasy."

Bobby whispered, "It was the horse to his outside, he was restless and that made FR nervous."

"That's what I am saying—we need to work out of the gate when we get home. That is one of the things that can really screw you up when you get into a race with a big field like the Derby may have."

"Stone, we are a long way from the Derby."

"Yes, Stone agreed. But you have at least three other races coming up, and you may face the same problem."

"Okay, Bobby said. You're the teacher."

Stone smiled and leaned his head back and closed his eyes. He had a dream about the Derby, and King-Flint. And afterwards, he and Angie had a candlelight dinner in their hotel room.

The plane landed, but Stone didn't want the dream to end.

. . .

They had three more races before the Derby, and FR won them all. None of them were as prestigious as the Graded Stakes races that his competition had been racing in, but they were all good races.

They just wanted to get him to the Derby as healthy as possible.

The Derby is one of the oldest and possibly the most prestigious race in America. Every owner, trainer, jockey, and three-year-old colt wants to compete in that race. It's a Chase for the Roses, referring to the blanket of roses draped across the horse after he wins the race. It is one of the most widely recognized days in sports across the country. People who don't ever go to a racetrack the rest of the year would make reservations months in advance just to be part of the pageantry and celebration. Beautiful Churchill Downs with the famous twin spires inspired songs and poetry. It causes everyone from little old ladies to multi-millionaire businessmen to get teary eyed with the singing of "My Old Kentucky Home."

Stone spoke of the race with awe, as did everyone who talked to Bobby about the event.

And it was with a racing heart that Stone began to think that this little colt of his beloved KingFlint actually had a chance to win. The horse and Bobby were like he and KingFlint had been. He would watch them work and feel a little envy that the kid was going to have a shot, the shot that he and his horse had not had.

But Stone loved this boy. He was everything a teacher could ask for in a student. He was happy every day just to be on the back of a horse.

And he felt such devotion to Stone that if he had told Bobby to ride off the edge of the earth, he and FlintRemembered would have disappeared over the edge.

Sandy and Stone were the two most important people in Bobby's life. He adored his wife and she adored him, but she knew that the love they had was not in any way second to his respect and affection for Stone. When she came to terms with that fact, she began to understand that there are a lot of rooms in our hearts, and even though she had a large portion of Bobby's heart all to herself, Stone had his own room there as well.

Bobby and Sandy loved the Dowd's too. They had become like a surrogate family to them and Sandy. Karen took Sandy under her wing and taught her to cook and to sew a little bit. She helped her decorate their home and was the confidant that Sandy talked to about everything. So it was just natural that Karen knew about the baby before anyone else.

Sandy wanted to tell Bobby right away, but he had a big race at the Fairground in New Orleans, Louisiana, and she didn't want to distract him for fear he would get hurt. She flew to Louisiana with him and was sick the three days they were there.

They came home, she went to the doctor for medicine for morning sickness, and he was able to give her something to help a little bit. Bobby was so busy working with FlintRemembered, and riding jobs all over the country that he hardly had time to eat much less realize she was not feeling well.

But, she wasn't going to be able to hide the news from him much longer. She was a small young woman and it wasn't long before her pregnancy started to show.

She waited until Bobby came home from riding FlintRemembered in a race at Belmont Park. He was in such high spirits, they had won the race and FR came back as healthy and feeling as good as he had from the other races.

Bobby told Sandy that he thought Don Dowd was a smart man before, and now the more he was around FR the more he was convinced that he was not just a good trainer but a great one.

Sandy had a nice dinner prepared and Bobby was just so happy to be home that he couldn't stop hugging her. For some reason every time he went to and returned from New York, he seemed extra happy to be home.

As the sat at the table, Sandy was quiet. She had rehearsed all afternoon what she would say, how she would tell him. But now that he sat across from her, she was at a loss for words.

They had often talked about having kids, later. Bobby wanted two and Sandy wanted four. Karen joked with her that she would change her mind after the first one.

"Are you okay, baby?" Bobby asked.

Sandy giggled and said, "That was a very good choice of words."

"What?" he asked.

"Baby," she said.

He held a forkful of food about halfway to his mouth, stopped, and looked at her.

"Sandy?" he said questioningly.

"Bobby," she said smiling.

He laid his fork down, got up, went around the table, and kneeled down beside her chair. He put his hand on her stomach and asked, "We're gonna have a baby?"

She smiled and said, "I hope it's okay, Bobby."

"*Okay* he yelled. Honey this is great! This is incredible!"

He raced to the phone and dialed his mother and Craig. After several minutes of celebration with them, he called the Dowd's (who already knew but pretended they didn't), then he called Aunt Iris who was shouting and so hysterical they couldn't understand her.

Sandy looked around and Bobby had run from the house to the bunkhouse and was telling Tom.

He wished he could tell Stone, but he would have to go to the Dowd's and find him. He always seemed to be with KingFlint and FR these days.

As soon as he was able to finish his dinner, Bobby and Sandy drove over to the Dowd's house.

Bobby ran to the barn while Sandy explained to them that he wanted to tell his horse. But Karen and Don knew the truth.

Stone was lying in a pile of hay outside the stall of KingFlint.

Bobby ran in yelling, "Stone! Stone! Where are you?"

Stone was on his feet and stood in front of him with a look of fear on his face.

"What's wrong, kid?"

"Nothing is wrong, everything is *right*, Bobby shouted. We are gonna have a baby!"

Stone grinned from ear to ear, "Well I'll be danged, he said. Another Tolliver kid to learn the racing game? That's wonderful news. Bobby, congratulations!"

Bobby said, "I have to go to the house. I will see you later, okay?"

Stone smiled and said sure and Bobby turned and started to walk away and ran back and grabbed Stone and hugged him. "I had nothing till I met you and Sandy. Now, I feel like I am on top of the world."

And he turned back around and ran like a little boy up to the Dowd's main house.

. . .

Life took on new meaning for them all. And Bobby, who had believed he had everything before the news about the baby, now felt like king of the world. But he also felt a sense of urgency to get more work and make more money.

So Stone suggested that Bobby get a riding agent and he talked to Greg O'Bryan, an old friend of Stone's from his riding days. Greg had retired young from riding and was working as an agent, and had gone on and finished law school as well. As soon as Bobby met him, he liked him. And the guy was good. In a very short time, he had every top trainer in the country wanting Bobby to ride for them.

Greg was good friends with a top California trainer, Benny Frank, and he convinced him to give the kid a shot on his top prospect in the Santa Anita Derby.

It was their first trip to California. Bobby was thrilled to get to ride at the great Santa Anita Race Track. Sandy was as excited as Bobby was about being in Los Angeles and they rented a car and went sightseeing. Stone had ridden in the Santa Anita Derby several times in his career and he shared a little of the history of the track with Bobby. Sandy couldn't get over the mountains in the background, and how different the Pacific

Ocean was from the Atlantic. Bobby won the race on the Benny Frank horse, TomsCoolery. It was not to be his last ride in California. He returned many times to ride at Santa Anita and also across town at Hollywood Park. Later in his career, he even rode in the Pacific Classic one summer at Del Mar.

Bobby was about to lose his apprentice weight allowance but no one seemed to care. Stone told Bobby some jockeys that had set the track on fire as "bugs" lost their edge when they lost their weight allowance. He was going to make sure that didn't happen to Bobby.

Stone was on every trip to every track. People had quit bothering him so much about the "Ghost Jock" as the Daily Racing Form had called Stone, and were taking note of the way the kid handled a horse.

He rode a lot more for Don Dowd than he did for anyone else. Don was his main man and there was no way he was going to turn him down if he needed him.

During a quiet time when he was back at home, waiting for the Keeneland fall meet to begin, Don called and asked if he and Sandy would come to dinner. This wasn't unusual, they were frequent guests at each other's homes. But something in Don's voice bothered Bobby. He hoped there wasn't trouble. Life was going too good for anything to come along and burst his bubble.

Don seemed edgy and nervous all through the meal. It was as if he couldn't wait for them to finish so he could talk to them about whatever was bothering him.

With dinner finally out of the way, he asked Bobby

and Sandy to go to the barn with him. Sandy looked at Bobby with a question in her eyes as they walked behind Don and Karen. He just shrugged.

When Don opened the office door at the near end of the barn, he turned and said to Bobby, "Remember the first horse you ever rode?"

Bobby laughed, "Well sure I do. NeverTardy, a nice little filly. Why?"

Don handed Bobby a piece of paper. He opened it and it read:

"Presented to Bobby and Sandy Tolliver for all their hard work, extra hours, extreme dedication, and duty above and beyond the call, Donald and Karen Dowd do hereby present to you our gift of one four-year-old filly named NeverTardy, out of the sire MajesticTime and the dam, AlwaysReady."

Bobby and Sandy stared with open mouths at Don and Karen.

"We wanted you to have a good mare to start your breeding with, and when Terry sold his interest in this filly, we thought she would be the perfect fit for your business."

"And, Don added. She is in foal to KingFlint."

Bobby was in shock.

Stone stood off from the four and whistled under his breath. "Kid, he said. He has just put you in the horse business."

Bobby said, "Don, Karen, I don't know what to say, this is just amazing."

Karen and Sandy hugged and then she hugged Don.

"Just a bonus for everything you have done, you have earned it."

"And, Don said. I felt like it was just right that King-Flint has made the full circle now."

"What do you mean full circle?" Bobby asked.

"That the last foal from KingFlint goes home. We are putting him out to pasture."

Bobby stared at Don with a blank look.

Don laughed, "Oh honey, he said to Karen. They don't know."

"Know what?" Sandy asked.

Don laughed again, "My family bought KingFlint from your grandfather, Bobby. I am sending him home. Well, the next generation anyway."

Sandy had tears in her eyes and she held Bobby's hand. "Oh Bobby, isn't that incredible?"

Bobby stood there in shock. "I had no idea," was all he could say.

They all walked to the stall where NeverTardy stood with her pretty head hanging over the half door. Stone was there already patting her and rubbing her face.

"She's a fine horse," he said to Bobby.

Bobby nodded. The lump in his throat made speaking to Stone or anyone else at that moment quite impossible.

Don would have nothing else but to trailer the filly and take her home right then.

As she walked into her new barn, Tom Cross smiled and said, "Well finally, I have a baby to take care of." The horse nuzzled his hand and everyone laughed.

THIRTEEN

As Bobby rode daily in the races at Keeneland, Stone watched and made mental notes. He would tell Bobby between races what he saw as he left the gate, how a certain horse reacted to the post position, and how they reacted to other horses in the field. And Bobby would remember.

In the third race on the second Saturday of the meet, Bobby was on a horse named ValorDays. He was a five-year-old running in a conditioned allowance race.

Bobby liked this trainer, Dick Carlton. He had hired him to ride a number of his horses. He always told Bobby to just ride the horse. And he would instruct Bobby on how this one or that one likes the lead or about the horse's quirks.

With ValorDays, he told Bobby to lay just off the lead and let the horse decide when he wanted to run.

Dick said the horse was very professional but didn't like the whip at all. He said, "Leave your stick here and ride him using your hands. If he sees the stick, he will go nuts on you."

This made Bobby a little uneasy since he had never ridden without a stick before. He asked Stone as Dick walked off to talk to his owner, "You ever ride without a stick?"

Stone said, "Yeah, but not too often, some horses just can't handle being hit. It's not the stick that bothers me, it's the way that guy is acting about it."

Bobby shook his head, "Well, I guess he's the boss, at least he didn't ask me to ride without a bridle."

"Or without pants, Stone added. But something about Dick's attitude makes me nervous today. He is just acting pretty weird."

Bobby laughed a nervous laugh, "Maybe he just has a lot on his mind, sometimes you really are a worry-wart."

When they brought the horses to the paddock for riders up, Bobby thought the horse seemed pretty lathered up and very nervous. He looked like he had already run a race.

When Bobby climbed aboard, the horse shied a little but Bobby spoke to him and the trainer grabbed hold of his bridle, slapped his nose, and said, "Quit it you fool."

Bobby handed his stick to Dick Carlton and rode the horse out to the track. As they began the post parade, the rider on the lead pony asked Bobby where his whip was. Bobby said the trainer told him no whip with this horse.

The rider said, "This horse has been a handful for the last three jocks that have ridden him.

I hope you aren't in for a wild ride."

Wild ride was an understatement.

The gate opened and the horse, coming out of the sixth hole, turned sharply to his right and bumped the seven and eight horses as they left the gate. He took off in a dead run straight down the backstretch, and then took another sharp turn to the right and ran along the fence row as if trying to scrape Bobby off his back.

Bobby was yelling at the horse and pulling back on the reins when his stirrups broke.

He was sitting on the horse like a bareback rider with no whip and no irons.

The horse was making a terrible strangling noise and as Bobby looked around, he could see the outrider about to gain on them. Bobby tried to calm the horse but ValorDays was determined to throw him off. As he saw the outrider's horse coming up on his outside, ValorDays began bucking like a rodeo bronco and it was all Bobby could do to stay on until the outrider was beside him. He slid over, grabbed the outrider's waist, and hung on until he pulled away from the crazy horse and Bobby slipped safely to the ground.

The ambulance was rolling up behind him as he sat down and shook his head.

He could hear Kurt Becker on the loudspeaker announcing to everyone that he was sitting up and appeared to be okay.

Bobby's first thought was that he was glad Sandy had decided not to fight the crowds today and had stayed home.

After the paramedics talked to him and determined that he was fine, he hitched a ride with them back to the stands.

The stewards still had the inquiry sign posted and Bobby had to go to the phone at the scales and speak to them. The stewards, who watch every race to make sure it is properly run, were questioning the way the horse behaved on the track. While Steward's Inquiries are very common, it was Bobby's first time to be involved in one with a horse going crazy on him.

Ted Barger, the Chief Steward, asked Bobby a few questions and then took the inquiry sign down.

Stone was waiting for Bobby as he walked back to the jockey's room.

"They had that horse juiced, he said angrily. That piece of dirt put you on a juiced up horse without a whip and poor equipment. It's a wonder that you didn't fall and seriously hurt yourself."

Bobby was angry, "I have some questions and I want some answers right now!"

He was on another horse in the very next race for Dick Carlton and he went to the paddock and called him to the side.

"Before I dress and get back on one of your horses, Bobby began. I want to know what happened with that one."

"Don't play smarty-pants with me kid, Carlton

yelled. You might think you are hot stuff, but there are a lot of jockeys that would love to ride for me. Something spooked the horse and he got away, that was all. Now get back in there and dress for this race!"

Bobby looked at him for a minute and then he walked away. He went to the jockey's room and put on the silks of the owner of Carlton's horse for the next race.

Stone said, "Bobby, if he asks you to do anything strange with this horse, you just walk off. You can always refuse to ride a horse you think is unsafe, and you can call for an investigation."

"I will be okay, Stone, Bobby said. I am not going to take any dumb chances."

The horse was in the paddock and Bobby walked over and saw Stone standing there rubbing his face. "He's all right, there had to be something going on with that other horse. This is not the same owner is it?"

Bobby shook his head.

"Dadgumit, sometime owners put so much pressure on trainers there's not much telling what Carlton did to make that horse act that way. It was speed of some kind for sure and it made him crazy instead of fast, but this guy looks and acts okay."

Bobby laughed, "He seems downright sleepy. Hope I can wake him up to get him out of the gate."

The race went off without a hitch, and his horse finished a respectable fourth. Carlton was happy and the owners were thrilled; it was the best the horse had done all year.

That had been Bobby's last race of the day and as

he went out to get in his car later, one of the Stewards was also leaving.

He waved at Bobby and then motioned for him to wait for him.

"Are you okay? We all held our breaths up there after that horse went whacko."

Bobby laughed and said, "Well, I had led a charmed life till then. I guess I was due one."

The Steward said, "Bobby we are going to ask for a blood test from that horse, in fact the track vet is probably drawing blood as we speak. Would you give us a statement later?"

"About what?" Bobby asked.

"Anything unusual happen with the horse or trainer before you took the mount?"

Stone said, "Tell him you will write your statement and bring it in. You better let Greg read it first."

"How about I write you out a statement and bring it in tomorrow?" Bobby asked.

"That would be great, we appreciate your cooperation."

Bobby smiled, shook his hand, got in his car, and drove home.

On the ride back to the farm, Stone said, "They will probably ask you to take a blood test too, that's pretty standard stuff. And if they do, then you will be off the hook with Carlton and it will look as if the Stewards looked at that incident themselves."

Bobby said, "Sure, I am not afraid of a little drug test."

The rest of the drive they chatted about Sandy and

the baby, but mostly they talked about the Derby and FlintRemembered.

Bobby had a call from Greg the next morning. He asked if he had written the statement yet.

Bobby told him that he was writing it as the phone rang, but that he wanted Greg to read it before he handed it in.

Greg told him that it was all a moot point; Carlton had written a note, left it on his dashboard, and had committed suicide right after the races.

Bobby was sick to his stomach. He felt like throwing up. He went to the barn and walked alone for a few minutes, wondering why someone would do something so terrible like commit suicide. A permanent end to a temporary problem.

It seems Carlton had injected the horse with enough speed to kill him. He had done it on his own he said, not out of fear or pressure from his owner. He absolved everyone involved of any wrongdoing. He was in financial trouble and needed the horse to win the race. He felt that if he hadn't won, the owner would be taking his horses to another trainer since they had not been doing well. He thought that getting the top jockey in the country to ride would give him some legitimacy. He said he honestly thought that Bobby would be able to handle the horse.

Stone was angry and said, "Stupid little man—gambles with your life because of money."

"Kid, he said to Bobby. When you are in this just for the money, get out! You lose your heart for the horses and for the game, get out! Go be a ditch digger or a bank president, but don't do it for any other reason than you do it now, for the love of the game."

Bobby nodded in agreement. "I won't Stone. The day I don't love it anymore, I am gone."

When Bobby told Don Dowd about the incident a few days later, Don felt a shiver go down his back. But he said nothing except, "Sometimes people do terrible things out of greed, Bobby. I am just glad you weren't injured."

. . .

They were three weeks away from the Derby, the baby was due any day, and the Kentucky weather was celebrating spring with sparkling clear skies and cool temperatures. The trees and fields were green, and early morning dew sparkled like diamonds on the ground.

Joy and Craig had come to Kentucky to spend the days before the Derby with them and be there for the baby's birth.

Sandy called her dad before they came and asked him to bring her some things from home. Sandy wanted to surprise Bobby when he came home from the track.

They had been working FlintRemembered with KingFlint as they had done a few times since taking him along that first time. Stone rode KingFlint and Bobby trotted along with FlintRemembered. It looked like Bobby was working his horse and letting KingFlint be the lead pony. But Don knew the truth and never said anything about it, because it truly was a thing of beauty to watch.

Bobby knew Sandy was up to something; she had a couple of contractors at the house for over a week, and Bobby knew they were working on one of the bedrooms to turn it into a nursery. So, he figured it was done and she wanted to surprise him.

She made him close his eyes and she led him down the hall.

"Okay, she said. Open."

She had turned a corner of the den into a study, and on one wall were framed pictures of him in the winner's circle on various horses. She had framed a front page from the Daily Racing Form with his caricature and *Bobby Phenom* written on a horseshoe shaped garland of flowers under the picture. She had his Apprentice Jockey of the Year Eclipse Award hanging beside that, and there were a few pictures of him as a child riding his horse here at the farm with grandfather in the background.

"And there is room for many more," she said.

He smiled at Sandy and said, "Wow, this is great!"

She turned him around and on another wall were some of the pictures of Stone that he had seen at Angie's house. There were pictures of Angie and Stone together, along with others of his horseracing pictures.

Bobby looked at his wife and she had tears in her eyes. "I thought you might like to share your success room with Stone."

He didn't say anything, he just reached over and

pulled her close. He leaned over and whispered in her ear, "I love you."

"Now, she said excitedly. Come see the nursery!"

Later that night as they lay ready for sleep, she rested her head on his shoulder and asked, "Do you think we will always be happy?"

Bobby laughed, "I wish I was a psychic and could answer that one for you honey, but no one knows what the future holds. If you are asking me if I will always love you, then the answer is yes. I knew the minute I laid eyes on you that you were the one for me."

Sandy asked, "You know what worries me?"

"What?"

"You have never done anything wild."

Bobby rolled over onto his side and looked at her. "I marry when I am just barely eighteen; I marry a girl who is not yet eighteen and take her away from her home. I bring her to Kentucky so I can chase roses, move her into an old ramshackle farm that I talked a bank into loaning me $100,000 for, I go all over the country like some modern day cowboy riding horses, and *that* doesn't seem wild to you?"

"I am just afraid that you will become bored with me and our life and want to sow some wild oats."

Bobby laughed, "Honey, the only oats I am going to sow are the ones out in that back pasture, and if I get a hankering to do something wild, I will do it with you, okay?"

She smiled, "Okay, fair enough."

Bobby leaned over and kissed and said, "I have

everything I ever wanted, Sandy. When grandfather died and mom and I lost everything, I thought my life was over. Then this pretty girl speaks to me on the beach and I felt a stirring in my heart, and I thought that maybe life was going to be okay after all. Look at me, barely twenty, married to the prettiest girl in the world, owning the farm I always loved, which by the way, my wife has turned it into a gorgeous home. We have our first baby due anytime, I get to do the job I wanted to do from the time I was six years old, and I have been taught by one of the best jockeys who ever lived. I don't know another person who can say that. Will we always be happy? Who knows, but we are happy now, and really, now is all we have."

FOURTEEN

Suddenly Sandy winced in pain. "Owww, that hurt," she said.

Bobby sat up, "Was that a labor pain?"

She nodded, "I think so, it was a pain that's for sure. Let's time them and see."

Bobby wanted to jump up and take her on to the hospital. It was a twenty-mile drive and he wanted to take no chances.

But Sandy assured him they would have plenty of time. She wasn't even sure she was having labor pains anyway, it was just *one* pain she told him.

She did get out of bed to go get a warmer gown, and her water broke. "Now, she said. Call the doctor and see what he says."

Bobby went to the guestroom and told their parents. Then he called the Dowd's so they could be prepared. Sandy wanted Karen with her in the labor room, she had made that very clear to everyone. Joy was very understanding about it. She and Craig had even taken to referring to Karen and Don as "the other grandparents."

It was a long night. They left for the hospital at 2 a.m. and Sandy delivered their beautiful baby boy at 8 a.m.

Everyone had been asking her what they were going to name the baby. She had only smiled and said, "We have to know what it is before we name it."

Now everyone in the waiting room was pressuring Bobby about a name. He said, "We haven't decided on a name. When we do, we will tell you."

Everyone left the hospital tired and ready for bed, except Bobby and Stone.

Bobby walked from Sandy's room after she fell asleep and saw Stone standing at the nursery window. He smiled when Bobby walked up.

"Well, Dad, he said. He's a fine looking boy. Lucky for you he looks like Sandy," and they laughed.

Bobby still got choked up when he looked at his baby. He was so tiny lying in the bassinet. He was sleeping with his little fist tucked under his chin.

"He's so small." Bobby said.

"They grow up fast. Enjoy him, he'll be grown before you know it."

"Stone, why didn't you and Angie have any kids?"

"We were planning to start a family, which was why we had decided to get married after the Derby. Getting married wasn't a big deal to either of us, we always knew we would. When we decided to try to have a baby, we wanted to be married first."

Stone turned his head away.

"I'm sorry," Bobby said.

"Just like I told you, kid—things don't always work out the way you plan."

Bobby shook his head. "Yep, I know. Life seems pretty unfair when you think about all of the 'could have beens.' I am going home and get some sleep, Bobby said. You want to ride along?"

"I think I will stay here a little while. Been a long time since I saw babies this tiny."

"I want you to see something at the house. Come by later, will you?"

"Sure," Stone said as he tapped the glass and smiled.

"Oh by the way, Bobby said as he stepped on the elevator. You don't have to call *him* kid. His name is Stone."

Stone didn't turn around for a moment and then he said, "What did you say?"

"You heard me, call him Stone." Bobby smiled and winked as the elevator door closed.

Later at his house, Bobby announced to the Dowds, Joy, and Craig that they had named the baby Stone. Don wasn't the least bit surprised when Bobby and Sandy announced the baby's name. He would have been surprised if they had not.

Stone was so touched, he had a very hard time keeping dry eyes and a straight face. He told Bobby that he couldn't imagine what the kid would have to go through with a name like that. Bobby assured him that he wasn't worried.

Stone came to the house that evening as he had promised and Bobby showed him the room that Sandy had made for him. He spent a long time looking at the pictures. Bobby told him that would always be his room.

. . .

Sandy and the baby came home from the hospital in two days. Karen and Joy helped out. As much as Bobby wanted to be there every moment and just stare at his son, he had a Derby to prepare for and other rides to ride. Don Dowd was taking all kinds of heat from other trainers, the public, and the media for not having raced FlintRemembered in a lot of the big races. The press had a field day with the few races he had run, calling him "FlintForgot, he forgot to show up." Don answered them all by saying that the colt had nearly died, he had lost months of training time, and had missed all the early spring races because of it. He had paid the supplement that was required and he felt like the colt deserved the chance to be in the Derby even if he hadn't danced at all the "important" parties.

Two horses, one named Cannon'sProspect and the other named DiagonAlley, were the two favorites. Diagon had won the Lane's End and the Arkansas Derby; Cannon had won the Wood and the Florida Derby. They seemed very evenly matched.

FlintRemembered had been working well, he was sharp and fit, and as soon as they took him to Churchill

Downs from Ellis Park, everyone remarked how much he resembled his sire.

Time seemed to fly by and Bobby was still winning races and occasionally taking heat from other jockeys. He wondered if he would always be remembered for thinking he could talk to a ghost rather than for his riding ability.

The day of the Derby, Bobby had a ride in four races. After the sixth race, as he and Stone sat outside the jockey's room, he said, "Stone, I wish you could ride this race. This should be your Derby."

"Well kid, you never know what's gonna happen, just enjoy *your* Derby. You've earned the right to be here. But don't be surprised at anything you see today, after all it is Derby day and wonderful things have been known to happen."

"What are you talking about?" Bobby asked him. But Stone just smiled.

"It still just doesn't seem right that you and King-Flint didn't get your shot. I wish..."and his voice trailed off.

Stone said, "Just ride your ride kid, your horse has a legitimate shot. Just pay attention, you never know what kind of surprise you might get." And Stone smiled again.

In the jockey's room, Bobby dressed in the Dowd's silks. He tied his tie and watched in the mirror as some of the other jockeys walked around, some sat and read, and others just stood off to themselves. Bobby looked up and saw Stone standing in the doorway dressed in the silks of Paul Dowd from 1975.

Bobby stared at him.

"Just for old time's sake," he laughed.

One of the other jockeys said, "Have a safe ride, Bobby." Then he turned to the other jockeys in the room and said, "Oh wait, he has no worries. He has angels, or ghosts or whatever watching over him, right?"

Bobby smiled and said, "Yep, that's right."

Phil Daily looked at the other guy and said, "Man, lighten up. This has worn pretty thin."

The other jockey shrugged and said, "Sure PD." And he walked off.

Phil smiled at Bobby and tapped his brow with his stick like a salute.

Bobby smiled back and said, "Thank you, Mr. Daily."

"God bless you, Bobby. Have a safe ride."

As Bobby stood in the paddock, he looked around at the other horses and ran through the field in his mind one more time. He knew them all by heart, he had memorized each one after the post position draw on Wednesday. He knew them. He had studied them. He knew who was a speed horse and who was a closer, he knew who would be running in the second tier of horses with FR. He knew everything he could know from statistics. Now he had to see if everything he had learned would pay off.

The horses and post positions:

- Cannon'sProspect. One of the favorites and a true speed horse. He liked to be alone on the lead, but had learned to run with company. He was a formidable foe.

- MysticPrince: Another speed horse.
- Eadie'sRisk: Speed
- Endeavor: He would be running along with FlintRemembered
- DiagonAlley: Dead closer, he would be running late with a huge kick.
- PietroCholco: Another closure but Bobby thought he was outclassed in this race.
- MigrantFarmer: Speed.
- MajesticMogul: Speed or could run off the pace with FR
- Jolie'sPeacock: Closer
- FlintRemembered: Just off the pace
- DallyDelay: Just off the pace with Flint. He was not quick enough to get past FR in the late stages though.
- Humbolt: Dead closer
- Jeehan: Late Scratch
- MaddDasher: Just off the pace.

All he had to do was maneuver FR inside to the rail and let him run his race. With this big field, it was Bobby's job to get him a good position, keep him out of traffic, and be clear when they turned for home.

In the paddock, Don stood as silent as a tree. He was nervous, so it was Karen who talked to Bobby.

"Bobby, just be safe out there, keep you and FR out of trouble."

Bobby smiled, "Believe me, we are gonna be out of everybody's way as soon as we can. I hope when we make that turn going into the stretch we will just be a dot on the horizon."

Karen smiled a nervous smile.

When they called for riders up, Don gave him a leg up and said, " Bobby, you know this horse better than anyone, you make the decisions, I trust you."

He shook Bobby's hand and walked alongside the horse until they reached the lead rider who took the reins from him and led FlintRemembered and Bobby Tolliver on to the great Churchill Downs track and their date with destiny.

Bobby looked back and saw Karen and Don holding onto each other for support.

The post parade went well. The crowd was noisy and boisterous. FlintRemembered didn't seem to pay attention to them he was so focused on the track.

Bobby talked to him as they walked along and then as they rode off to warm up.

"FR, we have been waiting for this day. Everything Stone has taught us has been for today. You are a good horse, you have good genes, good bloodlines, a good rider," and then he laughed.

The horse was very relaxed and loped around the track as if it was another workout.

As they neared the gate, Bobby began to feel his knees tremble. He swallowed hard, he couldn't let FR feel his anxiety. He could do this, they could do this.

Several of the horses balked at going in the gate, Cannon'sProspect being one of them. He was lathered up pretty good by the time they got him in the gate.

FR and Bobby waited their turn. The New York track announcer and voice of the Kentucky Derby, Tim Parks called their names as each horse was loaded.

FlintRemembered was the picture of good behavior as he walked right into the gate and stood perfectly still. The gate assistant told Bobby that he looked real nice.

Tim Parks made a comment as FlintRemembered was being loaded that his sire had run this race in 1975 and was also in the number ten hole. Bobby was surprised to hear that. He wondered why Stone hadn't told him they had the same post position.

Some of the horses were stomping their feet, very nervous in the gate. Tim Parks was telling the crowd that they were all just about loaded when the sound went off.

Even though you could hear the crowd, the noise wasn't as loud as it had been when they came out on the track. There seemed to be a power failure or something. The crowd was getting quieter. Everyone was looking around and wondering what was going on.

The starter spoke to someone on a walkie-talkie and yelled to the assistant starters to back the horses out of the gate.

Jimmy Colgin, the track vet, told the jockeys to dismount and let the lead ponies take their horses and keep them cool.

Bobby wondered what was happening. There were no lights, no voice of Tim Parks. It was eerie. The diamond vision screen in the infield was dark, and some of the other jockeys started asking Dr. Colgin if he knew what was going on.

Just as he started to speak, the diamond vision came on and the sound of a loud speaker began to crackle.

Bobby thought they had the problem fixed and started looking at the out riders to see if they were bringing their horses back.

A loud roar came from the crowd as Bobby heard a different announcer say, "And they are off!"

The crowd gasped with delight as the diamond vision and monitors all around Churchill Downs came to life with the ringing of the starting bell and twelve horses bursting from the gate. A replay evidently. Everyone was talking and laughing as the announcer called the order of the horses as they left the gate. It was a nice diversion right up until he called the name of the horse running second to last: KingFlint.

Bobby shook his head and thought he had to be hearing things. The announcer said, "Stone Hardaway is trying to keep KingFlint just off the pace, but his horse seems to be pulling at the bit trying to run."

Everyone in Churchill Downs watched a monitor in silence. The jockeys leaning against the fence walked over to the side nearest the stands where they could see the big screen.

The race was half over, they were about to make their turn for home and the long stretch drive to the Churchill Downs finish line. Bobby couldn't take his eyes off the screen. KingFlint and Stone were taking the lead as they went around the turn.

He wasn't even aware that he was yelling. He slapped the side of his leg and yelled, "Come on boy, come on!"

The silence was broken with the shouts of the crowd yelling and screaming for KingFlint.

Even the jockeys stood mesmerized as Stone Hardaway and KingFlint crossed the finish line first.

Bobby looked at the track, at the gleaming white fences and the finish line. The track was empty, except for the outriders and the lead ponies with the horses for the Kentucky Derby scheduled for this day in history.

Everyone watched as Stone rode KingFlint to the winners circle to Paul Dowd and the assistant trainer, and as the blanket of roses was draped across the neck of KingFlint.

Stone smiled and leaned over and patted his horse on the neck and the cameras flashed and people clapped. Stone jumped off the horse and took his tack to weigh in. He ran over to the group in the winner's circle and Bobby saw Angie standing there next to Stone.

His eyes scanned the crowd for Sandy. He knew she was close by; they expected to be in the winner's circle today and he had to see her face to see if she had watched what he and 60,000 people had just seen.

He saw her coming down a ramp from the box

seats where she had been sitting. She was wide-eyed, in shock—she and the rest of this enormous crowd.

A man standing against the rail spotted Bobby and yelled, "We owe you an apology, Tolliver. If you're crazy then we all are, 'cause I just seen Stone Hardaway win a Kentucky Derby when he was dead." Phil Daily walked over to Bobby. He didn't say anything, he just put his arm around his shoulder and patted him.

Everywhere Bobby looked, people were crying. The picture on the screen went black, then back to color and Tim Parks' voice could be heard again.

"Well folks, that was quite an experience. I don't know how to explain it."

The man who had yelled to Bobby looked up to the stands, "Shut up, Parks you idiot. We just saw that Kentucky Derby the way it should have been, there ain't no explaining to it."

FIFTEEN

Everything seemed to jump back into place, the horses came back, and the riders remounted and headed back to the gate.

No one spoke, not the jockeys, not the assistants, no one.

And no one looked at Bobby. At least not where he could see them. Tim Parks called for the horses to be loaded and started the process all over again.

As the last horse was loaded, the bell rang and Parks yelled, "And they're off!"

Twelve horses left the gate in a row and as expected Cannon's Prospect was the first to make the lead. Tony Darnell was riding him and he went straight for the rail.

The other speed horses tried to make a duel of it and were hard pressed to keep up with the speedy Cannon's Prospect.

As Bobby and FR settled on the rail just behind the speed, Bobby thought he heard Stone's voice.

"Just relax kid, relax, you got the best horse in the race. I hate to spoil your surprise, but you're not going to just win today—you and FR are going to take the Triple Crown."

Bobby shook his head and tried to stay focused on what he was doing.

Tim Parks was saying, "As they make the first turn Cannon'sProspect has a three length lead." And then he called the field with FlintRemembered getting a call from fifth.

Bobby had FlintRemembered in a good spot just off the pace, he was running easy and not in any hurry to make a move on the speed yet. Bobby could see that the two, three, and seven horses were already starting to tire. Cannon's Prospect seemed to be going easy, they hadn't set the really fast fractions Bobby thought they might. That might not bode well for the closers, especially DiagonAlley, who closed from out of the clouds and needed the pace to be faster than this.

Bobby heard Tim Parks say, "Cannon's Prospect has it his own way on the front end, but FlintRemembered has started to edge up and Cannon's Prospect's lead has been cut to two lengths. DiagonAlley has not geared up for his late run, he is still some seventeen lengths off these leaders. He had better start now if he wants to win this race."

It was then Bobby realized that he and FR were at the throat-latch of Cannon's Prospect. The speedster was trying hard to hold on, but FR hadn't even turned on his speed yet. Bobby looked over at his opponent and then asked FR to kick into another gear. Bobby heard screaming fans, and Tim Parks saying that FlintRemembered was going to win the race and everyone else was running for place money.

As they neared the finish line, Bobby dared to peek behind him and realized he had won the race by four or five lengths. Tim Parks said by six and who was Bobby to argue with the great Parks?

He stood in the stirrups, waved, and smiled.

As he galloped FR out another two furlongs, Bobby kept looking around trying to see Stone and KingFlint.

Suddenly, Donna Brothers, a television analyst, was riding alongside him holding a microphone to his face and asking him about the race.

He just wanted to get back to the winner's circle. Sandy was there. His baby was there and he wanted to hold them both, and he wanted to talk to Stone and find out what had happened.

As they trotted into the winner's area, Don Dowd ran out, grabbed Bobby's hand, and pumped it. "Great ride, Bobby. Just a fantastic ride." Everyone was there waiting for him, Sandy and the baby, his mother and Craig. Tom was there and even Aunt Iris had come up for the race.

He sat on the horse as they draped the blanket of roses across him. And he smiled as they took his picture on the horse, and again as they took more pictures in the winner's circle with everyone crowded around.

But he still didn't see Stone until he looked past the crowd and saw him leaning against the fence smiling.

There were hugs, handshakes, and kisses. Reporters were asking Don questions. But the big question from everyone was about the eerie race with Stone and KingFlint on television monitors that seemed to have been taken over by some outside force.

Bobby smiled as one reporter asked him if he felt like he was vindicated by the strange race.

"Me vindicated? Don't you mean doesn't Stone feel vindicated?"

The reporter asked Bobby if he could see Stone now and Bobby smiled and pointed to the fence.

Stone yelled, "Tell him I said he's about the lousiest reporter around because all he has done is write crap about you, and that I think he is a real jerk."

Bobby said, "Stone thinks you owe me an apology for writing some bad things about me being crazy."

"Don't forget the part about him being a jerk either," Stone said.

Bobby laughed and said, "Okay, Stone."

The reporters were scrambling around him, clamoring for him to talk to them and relay messages to and from Stone.

Bobby said, "I want to talk to my wife. Ask Stone these questions yourself." And he went over to where Sandy stood with the Dowd's and the rest of the family.

The reporters looked at each other, the empty spot at the fence, and walked away.

One of the newsman asked Sandy about the baby.

She told him he was a boy and was born three weeks before the Derby. When asked the name, she smiled and said, "It's Stone, we named him Stone."

The newsman immediately started to ask another question. But Craig leaned over and said, "This is a happy day, that's enough questions."

The newsman smiled, nodded, and walked away.

Sandy told him she, Karen, and the baby would see him later at the party. He kissed her, leaned over, and kissed the baby's head.

"I want you to tell me what happened this afternoon, Bobby, but later tonight when we are by ourselves."

"I hope I have an answer for you, honey."

Karen hugged him and told him how proud she was and he thanked her for everything they had done for them. She remarked, "You have done more for us than we have ever done for you!"

Bobby walked to the fence and said to Stone, "Now, what just happened out here?"

Stone smiled, "What a ride, huh?"

"Stone?" Bobby asked questioningly.

"KingFlint had his shot thanks to you and Flint Remembered. I knew he could win it if he had a decent ride."

Bobby stared at Stone. "You mean that happened?"

Stone nodded.

"Well there's something else to keep me awake nights wondering about," Bobby said with a small laugh.

"Kid, I can't explain it to you. It has something to do with right and wrong. Fixing a wrong or making something right, I don't know how else to say it. We rewrote the history book today, but we wrote it the way it should have been."

Bobby shook his head and held up his hand. "I don't want to know, I really don't. All I know you have taught me more in a couple years than I could have learned on my own in a lifetime. For whatever reason you were sent here I will always feel blessed for it and for the chance to get to know you. The Preakness and Belmont are next, you are with me aren't you?" He was afraid of the answer.

"Nope, this was my final ride, kid. You don't really need me anymore anyway. You wanted to be a great jockey and you are one. You proved that. You ride with heart and a natural ability, all I did was help you tighten it up a bit."

Bobby had tears in his eyes. "I don't want you to go. I *do* still need you around."

Stone smiled. "I have a date with an angel, kid. You don't want me to keep her waiting, do you?"

Bobby lowered his head and said, "No, I guess I don't."

"You are destined for great things, kid. I am the lucky one to have been here with you for a while. Take care of the little kid…I mean…Stone….and Sandy. And don't worry, I'll keep an eye on you."

He reached over, patted Bobby on the shoulder, looked at him for a minute as if to make sure he never forgot his face, then without a look back, he disappeared into the crowd.

Bobby called out after him., "Stone wait, wait a second." But he was already in the throng of people that were milling around. As Bobby stood there watching, Angie walked out of the crowd and took Stone's hand. She looked back at Bobby and smiled and then she and Stone disappeared into the crowd.

. . .

Bobby stood there and watched the people until Don came over and said, "Come on, Bobby. Let's go find our girls, and on the way you can tell me if you saw the same thing I did today."

Bobby took one more look into the crowd and walked away.

Don asked him what he had made of the weird blackout and Stone's ride on KingFlint.

Bobby shook his head. "I only know one thing, Don. Stone Hardaway has gotten his redemption for KingFlint. He was always so outraged by the sense of injustice that he felt was his fault, that now maybe he can find some peace."

Don looked at him quizzically, "What injustice?"

"He felt like his dying kept KingFlint from winning the Kentucky Derby. So today they got their ride and they did it in front of a crowd that I guess sort of symbolized the people that have given me so much grief over thinking that he was really here and I could see him. Today, everyone did. So, if I am crazy, they are too." And he laughed a sad laugh.

Don shook his head. "Well, that sounds like Stone Hardaway, may he rest in peace."

Bobby smiled. "He had a date with an angel. I think he's gonna be fine."

Bobby and FlintRemembered did go on to win the Triple Crown just as Stone had said they would.

The Dowd's business grew with the help of two Triple Crown winning stallions standing at stud, and Bobby continued to ride for the Dowd's and other top trainers around the country.

SIXTEEN

Sandy and the children, five year old—about to be six if you asked him—Stoney and four-year-old Emma, were in the supermarket shopping.

Emma liked riding in the basket so she was almost face to face with her mom. Stoney walked alongside the basket and helped Sandy when she found something she wanted.

They were laughing and talking. Sandy was trying to find something special to cook. Bobby was coming home after a long road trip to New Orleans, riding at the Fairground.

Emma asked, "Will daddy still look like daddy?"

Stoney grimaced. "You are such a dope, Emma. Sure he will look like Daddy"

"Don't call your sister a dope, Stoney, that's not nice. Yes, Emma, daddy will still look like daddy."

Emma was about to speak when she looked shyly at the man standing beside her mother.

Sandy looked over at the man and smiled. Then she pushed the basket on down the aisle.

"Who was that man?" Stoney asked.

"I don't know honey, why?"

"Cause, he's following us."

Emma didn't like the man, she stuck her tongue out at him.

"Emma! Sandy exclaimed. What in the world—" Just as she was about to finish her sentence, the man walked along beside her.

"You're prettier than ever, Sandy."

She stopped the basket and looked at him. There was something vaguely familiar about him, and some thing very disturbing too.

"Do I know you?" she asked him.

"It's me, Matt Stanley. Remember my Uncle Max? He sold you your house."

Sandy thought for a minute and then she remembered why she was disturbed.

"Oh yes, I do remember, how are you? We were sorry to learn that Mr. Stanley had died."

"Yeah thanks, me too. He was my last living relative. Isn't that something to think about, no one left in your whole danged family?"

"Yes it is, but please watch your language in front of the children."

He didn't seem to hear her, or didn't care, he just looked around and said, "How come ole Bobby ain't here with you? He didn't go off and leave his pretty little wifey alone, did he?"

Sandy said nothing, she pushed the basket off down the aisle.

He limped up to walk beside her.

"That place where you live was supposed to belong to me. Uncle Max promised me he was leaving it to me in his will. The danged old coot lost all his money and had to sell it, and I was out, and Bobby Tolliver was in."

Sandy tried to ignore him, but he followed them, talking about how he had been cheated. Sandy stopped her shopping cart and said, "Really, your family business has nothing to do with us. Your uncle told my husband after his grandfather died that he would sell it to him anytime he wanted to come back and buy it. I think you are just dreaming."

Stoney noticed him limping and he asked, "What happened to your leg, mister?"

Sandy said sternly, "Stoney, that's very impolite."

"No matter, he's a kid, he has a right to ask a question. How you ever gonna learn about the jerks in your family is if someone doesn't tell you?"

Sandy stopped the basket again and put her hands on her hips. "I have heard about enough from you, Mr. Stanley! You broke your leg and hip after you stole a horse! Now how would our family have anything to do with that?"

Matt started to speak and she said, "I don't care to hear anything else from you! Come on kids, let's go."

She pushed the basket to the checkout counter and he started to follow her.

She turned and said, "If you take one more step toward me...*ever*. I will call the police, do you understand?"

Matt smiled a sinister smile and said, "See you around."

"No, you won't see me around."

"I'll be watching you...you know, just to make sure you're safe when Bobby is gone; that's the least I can do for an old friend."

"Don't even think about it you jack—oh for heaven's sake, you just infuriate me, stay away from us!" And everyone in the area stopped and looked at her and at Matt.

Emma was wide-eyed in the buggy and Stoney was tight-lipped and shuffled his feet nervously.

"That man almost made mommy say a bad word," whispered Emma.

"Oh, hush, Emma."

The children were quiet on the ride home. Sandy kept checking her rearview mirror, certain that every car behind her was his.

She was happy to see Hopsend Road and the big swinging gate to the driveway.

After she pulled in, she got out of the car and pulled the gate closed and latched it. Something they never did.

The kids never asked her why.

She was happy to see the dogs on the porch. Danny was getting old so they had adopted another big German Sheppard and named him Darwin. Both dogs ran to the car, dancing excitedly to see their family home at last.

After the groceries were carried in, Sandy locked the car and put both dogs in the house.

She wandered out to the barn to see Tom. He was busy looking after the horses. She debated whether to tell him about Matt Stanley or not and decided at last not to say anything.

Tom had begun staying in town with his daughter at night sometimes. Her husband had been killed in a boating accident a few months prior and she was still very distraught and needed help with the kids. He told Sandy he was leaving about dark to go to her house.

Sandy didn't realize she had made a face when he told her, and he immediately picked up on something being wrong.

"Okay," he said. "What's up?"

"Nothing, just ready for Bobby to be home, that's all."

Tom looked at her for a minute and then he said, "What's really eating at you?"

"Nothing, nothing, I am okay. I think I am just tired. Seeing shadows, that's all."

"Okay, but if you need me, you call I am just six miles away."

"Thanks, Tom. I will, and we are fine, really."

. . .

She watched from the window as Tom drove out of the driveway. She pulled the curtains closed and said to the kids, "Guess what? I think we will have a slumber party tonight, you and the dogs can sleep with me, won't that be fun?"

The kids acted like it was a party, but they knew Mommy was scared.

Bobby saw his family waiting for him as he walked from the airport. They always parked on the curb, so they could make a hasty getaway. Today they were standing on the sidewalk waiting for him. He grabbed them all, hugged, and kissed them.

Sandy clung to him and he knew immediately that something was wrong. He tilted her face up to his and kissed her, and for a long moment, he stared into her eyes. He could see the tears welling up and he whispered in her ear. "I am home, everything is going to be okay."

She nodded and handed him the keys to the car. He was surprised, usually she drove home so he could play with the kids on the ride.

But he said nothing, just went to the driver's side and they took off for home.

It wasn't until the kids were in bed asleep that they had a chance to talk.

Sandy sat beside him on the couch and they talked about his trip and where he was off to the next time. He had Kentucky for the next few months much to Sandy's relief. He didn't have the heart to mention that he was going to ride another Derby horse for Don Dowd and then it was off to Maryland and New York if all went well. That was down the road; for now he was here and would get to sleep in his own bed for a while.

Sandy wasn't sure whether to even tell him about Matt Stanley or not. She didn't know how he would react. But she couldn't keep it to herself so she told him about the whole incident.

His face barely changed expression as she talked. And then he said, "If that creep ever comes around here, even steps foot on this property, I want you to get that shotgun and shoot him, Sandy."

She looked at him with shock. "Shoot him? Bobby I can't shoot anyone, I couldn't shoot him, I wouldn't be able to."

"Well, consider the alternative—he gets in the house and hurts you or the kids."

"The dogs are great protection, they wouldn't let him *in* the house."

Bobby shook his head. "And if he manages to put them out of commission?"

Sandy was quiet, then she sighed, "He hurts my dogs, I will shoot him."

Bobby laughed quietly. "I am getting security put in here. Don has been talking about the same thing for a long time."

"Well, that might help," Sandy replied.

They finally went to bed but Bobby didn't sleep for a long time. He tried to make a plan about security; maybe even video cameras for the gates and around the house. It was very late when he finally fell asleep, and for the rest of the night he fought faceless forms trying to get in the house.

Things were quiet in their life again. Bobby was home and all was well. Sandy and the kids went back to the store many times and never saw Matt Stanley again. And before long, the whole incident was forgotten.

SEVENTEEN

One week after the Kentucky Derby, which Bobby and the Dowd horse did not win but placed second, Karen Dowd was back home in the kitchen talking to her sister on the phone.

She sat at the little table in the corner of the kitchen and stared out the window at the birds and the squirrels giving their dog a fit.

Something caught her eye and she looked over to the barn area just in time to see Bobby Tolliver go in the big barn where FR and KingFlint were stabled.

She looked for his truck and wondered why he hadn't come to the house. She was certain Don had sent him for something and so she went on with her conversation.

It wasn't until a while later that she heard the cries of the hired hands and looked to see the barn on fire.

It was an intense fire, burning quickly with all the hay and seed they had stored in it. She screamed for them to get the horses out while she dialed the fire department and Don.

She saw the men racing around trying to get water hoses on it, and then she saw that a couple horses were out and tied to trees, and the men were fighting flames trying to get back in the barn.

The fire trucks arrived and it was chaos and confusion.

Don and Bobby pulled up and ran toward Karen at the barn. It was now a smoking, smoldering pile of rubble.

"What happened?" Don yelled.

She tried to explain that she had been in the house and that everything was fine. She said, "You were here, Bobby. Everything was fine. Did you see anything when you went in there?"

Bobby looked at her strangely. "What are you talking about Karen? I haven't been here today, we have been at the track."

Don nodded, "What are you talking about honey? You saw someone?"

The fire captain came over and said, "Well, we have this one under control, but whoever set it sure wanted everything to burn fast."

Don shook his head again. "What are you saying, Jim, is that someone intentionally set my barn on fire?"

Jim nodded, "Set it with gasoline and octane booster."

Bobby, Karen, and Don looked at each other. "Who would want to do something like that? Karen asked.

One of the hired men came over to the group and was crying. "Mr. Don, KingFlint, he didn't make it."

Karen gasped, "Oh no!" And she took off running to the house.

Don turned and without a word went racing back to the barn. Bobby followed behind not sure what to expect.

Bobby stopped at the edge of the barnyard and watched as Don went over to the body of the old horse. He kneeled down and stroked his head.

All of the hired men were crying, but Don had his back to Bobby and he couldn't tell if he was crying or not. In his heart, he knew he had to be. KingFlint was the star of the Dowd's farm. Even FlintRemembered didn't hold as special a place for them as the old horse did.

Bobby walked toward Don slowly, and he was relieved to see that the horse hadn't been burned.

Don was talking to the fireman that had squatted down beside him. Bobby heard him tell Don that the old horse had just keeled over after the hands got him out. "It had to have been a heart attack, Don. He just couldn't take it."

Don nodded and then he stood up and told the hands to get a hole dug for them to bury KingFlint. He pointed to a shady pasture and as he wiped his eyes, he said softly, "He loved to stand there under those trees and think. If any of the other horses wanted anything to do with him they had to come to him, he would just stand there like the King that he was."

He told Martin the foreman to take care of whatever they needed to make the grave a safe one. No wild animals digging on KingFlint's grave.

He patted Bobby on the arm and said, "Well, now that Stone has his horse in heaven with him, I guess they can ride together forever."

Bobby choked back a sob. He hadn't even thought about Stone through all this. His eyes scanned the backyard and the barn area for a sign of Stone, but there was nothing. He walked to the house with Don to check on Karen.

They found her sitting on the couch, the house almost dark. Don went and sat down beside her and they collapsed into each other's arms. Bobby shuffled his feet for a minute and then he walked from the room. He needed to see Sandy and hold her, and tell her what had happened.

Sandy cried when Bobby told her about the fire and about KingFlint. The kids were playing in the living room and they stood wide-eyed as they watched their parents consoling each other, neither child understanding what had happened.

. . .

Almost before light the following morning, Don Dowd was in the Tolliver's driveway pulling a horse trailer.

Bobby wiped the sleep from his eyes and went out to meet Don.

"What's going on, Don?" He asked.

Don was busy opening the trailer door and he said, "I brought FR over here to stay with you. You can use him with your mares if you want to."

Bobby laughed, "Hey, I can't afford FR's stud fee right now, maybe when he's older and the ladies aren't all lined up for him."

Don smiled and said, "I am going to have to ask you to let the ladies dance with him here, that's why I am giving you the opportunity to let *your* ladies dance with him while he's here."

Bobby swallowed hard, "You're joking, right?"

Don just shook his head.

"How many dates does he have for this month?"

Don kicked the gravel and said, "About one a week. He has been pretty popular. And tomorrow I plan on bringing SillyAngel, CapriCode, and Laffy over if you don't care. Just till we get the barn rebuilt."

"Sure, we have plenty of room. No problem, Don."

"I will send the guys over to help take care of things. Old Tom can ramrod the outfit as he sees fit, but that's too much work for him to do alone."

Bobby smiled, "Thanks, that's great. Nothing Tom likes more than bossing people around. Unless it's spoiling my kids."

After the trailer was unloaded and Don had gone home, Bobby walked around in the barn and talked to FlintRemembered.

"Well, I am gonna get to have some FR's too…man, that's unbelievable. After NeverTardy had TheKingsNvrLate, I wondered how long we would have to wait before we had another superstar."

He stood at the stall gate and scratched the horse's nose. Without thinking, he reached in his pocket and handed him a peppermint. The horse took it and snorted. Bobby laughed. "You're welcome boy. That's a trick my buddy Stone taught me."

Suddenly, grief gripped Bobby like a heart attack. He hadn't had time to think much about Stone in the past few years. Oh sure every time he walked past a picture on the wall, or did something at the track that reminded him of all the time he had spent learning with him, Stone crossed his mind. But he hadn't thought about how much he missed him and how he wished he could see the farm and the kids.

Sandy came out of the house, walked up behind Bobby, and put her arms around his waist. "Whatcha doing out here? Hey, what's FR doing here?"

Bobby told her about Don.

"We get to breed the mares to him? Wow, that's very generous of Don."

"He has always been so good to us. We are the kids he never had...well, you know what I mean," Bobby said. Sandy nodded.

"I was thinking about Stone just now, Bobby told her. Wishing he could see the kids, and the place. Just missing him."

Sandy said softly, "I read this quote from Thomas Campbell. It always reminds me of Stone and Angie. 'To live on in hearts we left behind, is not to die.'"

Bobby smiled at her and said, "Then those two will live forever, won't they?"

She smiled and nodded.

They walked arm in arm to the house to get the kids up and make breakfast.

Bobby didn't see the figure hiding in the trees just off the property. Watching as Sandy slipped her arm through her husbands and laugh as he kissed her. The dark figure frowned and spit on the ground and limped off into the dark woods.

. . .

Bobby and the Dowd horse DancingHerman won the Preakness Stakes, knocking the Derby winner out of a chance to take the Triple Crown. Sandy and the kids stayed in Kentucky rather than going to Maryland. Bobby told her he would not stay over, he would just fly in for the day to ride, and then fly right back out and be home before dark.

But severe afternoon thunderstorms snarled freeway and air traffic and he was grounded until morning. He thought about renting a car and driving home, but it was a long drive, and he would accomplish nothing. He still wouldn't be there with his family that night.

Sandy took the news better than he expected. She tried to reassure him that they would be safe. And she said Tom had agreed to stay there with them, so they wouldn't be alone.

Bobby felt better after he heard that Tom was staying.

But all night he tossed and turned as the storms raged outside, his heart raced within.

The storms spread all across the eastern coast, including Kentucky as they streamed across from the west.

Sandy was wide-awake too as the wind blew and the rain pelted the roof. She felt safe with the storm. No one would come out on a night like this.

The kids were in bed with her and they were sleeping soundly. Both dogs slept peacefully at the foot of the bed. Only occasionally poking their heads up when a big crack of thunder rattled the glass.

She tried to sleep, but her mind was restless. She tossed and turned until morning.

The day started off bright and sunny, but storm clouds still gathered around and she felt tired to the bone.

After she got the kids out to play, she laid down on the couch to nap. And she fell into a restless sleep.

Emma's screams woke her.

EIGHTEEN

Bobby and Don found a ride back from Maryland with an owner who was heading to Kentucky to check on some horses that would be in the next auction.

Bobby couldn't eat and was having a hard time sitting still. After what seemed an eternity, the private jet landed and Don and Bobby walked off the plane and saw Karen waiting for them.

She tried to explain to them what was being done so far, but it didn't seem like anything to Bobby.

When they pulled into the yard, Sandy and Emma ran to Bobby and he held them close.

Bobby talked to the FBI and then he asked Emma to show him where she and Stoney had been.

As they climbed up the old steps to the hayloft, Bobby felt a stabbing pain in his heart. If he had only been here. Sandy would probably never forgive him.

They sat on the hay in the loft as Emma recalled what had happened.

Bobby had never been a very religious man, but he said aloud, "Please Lord, please take care of our little boy."

Sandy said, "Amen."

Emma watched her parents and then she folded her hands and said, "Now I lay me down to sleep, I pray the Lord my soul to keep, if I should die before I wake, please bring Stoney home. Amen."

Bobby and Sandy both said, "Amen."

Don walked into the barn and called Bobby. He slid down the pole while Sandy and Emma went back down the ladder.

Don said, "They think someone spotted the truck in Tennessee."

Bobby took off running to the house.

Agent Sharp said as soon as Bobby opened the door, "It's an unconfirmed sighting, I have no idea how he would have made such good time. What we do want is for you two to go on national TV and ask this guy to bring your boy home. Promise him anything, ask him to call and let you know that Stoney is okay."

There were TV crews already setting up outside the house, the national press was there, and everyone was clamoring for an interview. Bobby and Sandy stood with Emma between them and begged Matt Stanley to bring Stoney home.

"Just call and let us talk to him. Please just let us know he is safe. And tell us what you want," Bobby pleaded into a maze of cameras and microphones.

After they finished the television segment, they excused themselves and went inside and talked to Agent Sharp. After Bobby got Sandy asleep on the couch he decided to take a walk. He had to do something; this helpless feeling was more than he could stand.

Sandy and Emma were both asleep; and Agent Sharp was conferring with a couple of men from the Sheriff's office. As he started to walk away, Bobby thought he should tell him he was going for a walk, but decided not to say anything, he was afraid Sandy would wake up and he was sure she would not want him to leave. But the fresh air felt good in his lungs, and he hoped it would help clear his head. He just wanted to try to think like Matt would think.

Bobby wandered off behind the barn and toward the back pasture. The land that joined his was wooded and dense with underbrush for several hundred yards, then it opened up to beautiful pastureland, dotted with big trees and gently rolling hills. He thought to himself that after this was over, and Stoney was home safe, he was going to buy this land and put some nice riding horses and cows on it. As he stared off in the distance, something caught his eye. It was the late afternoon sun reflecting on a piece of metal. Bobby struggled through the underbrush and worked his way toward the reflection. As he clamored through the trees, he thought could see the front part of a truck's bumper behind the old shed that had once housed tractors and mowers.

He was positive something was there. It was too shiny to be an old tractor part.

. . .

Matt hadn't been listening to the radio or television to hear the Tolliver's plea for Matt to return Stoney. He, Stoney, and FR were in the barn that Bobby was just about to walk up on.

Matt had been staying at the barn for weeks. This was an easy hideout, easy to get to the Tolliver's through the back pasture where he could stake out the house and watch Sandy.

Man she is a beauty, he often thought. *What the heck did she see in that wimpy little Bobby Tolliver?*

After watching the Tollivers for a time, he had decided that the best way to get rid of Bobby was to get him in trouble. But burning the Dowd's barn had backfired. He had not known that Bobby was with Don Dowd that day. He didn't know anything about horseracing and he didn't know it was not a racing day, that they were at the track for just a while to work out some horses and then they would be back. He had made certain that people saw him, he was even dressed in Bobby's old pants and hat he had stolen from the Tolliver barn.

One of the old Mexican hired hands had even waved at him, and he could have sworn that Old Lady Dowd saw him from the window of the house. But that plan failed and now they would have him for arson as well as kidnapping.

The old barn faced east with windows on the north and south side. Matt had covered the windows so he could have lights but no one would be able to see them. There was an old shed across the driveway and he hid the truck in there. The trailer was in the back of the shed. He had all the comforts of home. But everything was going wrong.

Matt slapped the door facing and then looked over at Stoney. What had ever possessed him to take this kid? He was only going to steal the famous racehorse and then this kid played Superman and he had no choice but to throw him in the truck.

Stoney had been very quiet, only talking when Matt said something to him. He did tell him that his daddy would get Matt when he got home. Matt had laughed and Stoney quit talking, just to keep from crying.

Matt walked over to the chair where Stoney sat. "Are you hungry, kid?"

Stoney shook his head.

"Better eat something. We are going to be here a long time."

Stoney sat perfectly still and didn't look at Matt.

Matt stared at him a minute and then said, "Fine, suit yourself."

He went over and stood in front of FR's stall. Well, at least we got a Triple Crown winner in our presence, Big Shot horse. He glared back at Stoney. Big shot horse and little snot kid." And then he laughed at his joke.

He went to the window of the barn and opened it a crack.

He didn't figure anyone would be looking for them this close. He had called the Highway Patrol disguising his voice to sound like a woman and reported he saw a truck matching his description near the border of Tennessee. He laughed to himself as he thought about the dumb cops and FBI looking all over the country for them and here they were, right next door. Right under their stupid noses.

There was nothing in sight, and Matt closed the window and went back to his seat across from Stoney's chair.

"So, what grade you in, Junior?"

Stoney stared at him in silence.

Little smart punk, aren't you? I bet you'll be talking in a while, once you get hungry and miss your mommy. But hey, I miss your mommy. I like watching her from the woods. And when this is all over and your daddy is out of the picture, she will want me to take his place."

Stoney wanted to hit him with something, but he sat still.

"Yep, I am gonna take over the reins of that pretty little filly Sandy Tolliver. I knew she wanted me that day in the store. She was mad because she had you kids with her and she had to play it cool."

"You liar! Stoney shouted. My mommy thinks you're a....a.....*pig*!"

"Sit down, you little brat! You don't know anything about men and women. When a woman says no she means yes, I could see it in her eyes. I am gonna be your new daddy, you'd better be nice to me."

Stoney jumped up, ran over, and started hitting him with his fists. "Liar, liar, my daddy will kill you! You better run away before he finds you!"

Matt restrained the sobbing Stoney and made him sit in his chair. He took some cord and tied Stoney's hands behind his back.

"Now, let's see how you like that, Mr. Wise Guy!"

Matt walked over to the sliding door of the barn and opened it a crack to get a look from a different angle. It was getting late in the day. Just as he was certain they were alone in the woods, Matt felt the force of Bobby Tolliver's fist as it hit him squarely in the mouth.

Stoney screamed, "Daddy, Daddy, I knew you'd come for me. I knew you would!" Bobby looked over to where his son sat tied to a chair and was about to speak just as the wooden board came around and hit him on the side of the head. The force from Matt Stanley's swing knocked Bobby out cold.

Matt's mouth was bleeding as he dragged Bobby to a stall beside FlintRemembered and tied his arms to the gate. He threw Bobby's head back and opened his eye to make sure he hadn't killed him. Then he turned around to an ashen-faced Stoney and said, "One loud word from you, kid, and I will cut his throat."

Stoney wept softly in his chair.

The evening settled on Kentucky like a dark shroud and Matt took his flashlight and shined it around the barn. He didn't like the darkness, but he couldn't have too much light in here just in case some cop was out there nosing around. And now that he had Bobby in here too, he was pretty sure the cops would be coming around. Why couldn't Bobby have stayed in Maryland? Or at home with his wife?

Now Matt had the kid, the dad, and a horse. And he was stuck here in this creepy barn for yet another night. What he was really afraid of was snakes and rats. And there were always plenty of both in a nasty barn. He shined the light around the barn floor and then in Stoney's eyes.

"You scared of snakes or rats, little brat?"

Stoney stared at him with blinking eyes. "I am not afraid of snakes or rats, not even a big rat like you, he shouted at Matt. And when my Dad wakes up, he will let you have it!"

Matt laughed a cruel laugh. "Well you better help me keep an eye out for snakes, 'cause I don't like them, and I don't like you either. And old dad ain't gonna help nobody kid, he's out for the night and I got him tied up tighter than...well, let's just say, he ain't going nowhere...I was just gonna get rid of you, but I think I should be the hero that brings you back home to your momma. She will be so thankful that she will tell your dumb daddy to get lost—neither he nor the cops could find you, but good ole Matt brought you home safe and sound. Then she will be mine. Women are real suckers for heroes, you know that?"

Stoney was relieved to hear he had no plans to hurt him, but intended to take him home. He just wished it were tonight.

"My momma wouldn't want you if you brought her the whole planet. And you're a dope cause she loves my Dad. She won't ever take you over him."

Matt laughed, "We shall see, we shall see. Then his

mood turned dark and he said, "Maybe I should just hang you and make it look like an accident. Or I could shoot you; my momma killed my little brother, did you know that? She was going to kill me too, but I ran away and hid. Now I got your dear old dad to take care of too."

Stoney said nothing. The barn was completely dark now and he couldn't see Matt's face. At least Matt had stopped talking to him. He was very quiet. Matt was breathing, Stoney could hear him breathing, almost like he was asleep. Kind of like snoring.

Sure enough, the flashlight fell into the hay on the floor and Stoney felt very alone. He stared over at his dad, but it had become so dark that he couldn't even see his face. He just hoped he was all right.

He tried to lean his head back against the wall but he kept thinking about home, and then about snakes and rats, and he was too afraid to sleep. It was a very long night.

Matt slept about three hours and awoke with a start. He felt around for the light and then shined it in Stoney's face to make sure he was still there.

NINETEEN

Stoney was blinded by the light. Matt got a lot of pleasure from shining it in his face and then turning it off and then shining it again and again. He laughed as he tormented Stoney until the flashlight went flying from his hand as if someone had slapped it from him.

"Hey!" he shouted at the darkness.

The light was on and he went to the corner of the barn and got it and shined it around the room and then at Stoney again.

"Did you do that you little—?" Stoney looked at him blankly.

Matt shined the flashlight over to the stalls where he had Bobby tied up, and Bobby's head was drooping on his chest, so Matt was sure Bobby was still out cold.

Matt sat down and fumbled with the flashlight and then he said, "I have decided I am not going to go back for your mother. Too many cops looking for me. I just have to get rid of you, your dad, and that stupid horse, and get away to Mexico. I could send for your mother when I am settled there, but I might find myself a pretty little senorita and not care about her anymore. Yeah, a pretty senorita that does anything I say and can't talk back to me. When daylight comes, I am gonna shoot that horse...oh dang, I can't shoot it, the sound of gunfire really carries in the woods. You I can hang, I will just leave the old nag and let him starve to death. And I will let your dad watch me hang you and then I am going to...well...I haven't decided how to do away with him yet, but I am certainly going to make sure he gets to watch you die."

Stoney said, "You won't ever make it to Mexico, and if you did they will make you come back here and die for killing us."

"You sure are a know-it-all little twerp, Matt said sarcastically. I won't ever be found in Mexico. I have Uncle Max's little dab of money he left me. It's a lot in pesos. I can live real nice."

Stoney couldn't make out Matt's face yet, but he knew he had a crazy gleam in his eye. Stoney had been thinking that if anyone ever talked to him for very long, they would see he was crazy. And now he was scared.

"Why don't you just leave us here too? Leave us here with FR and then you won't be a killer?"

"Maybe I want to be a killer," Matt said.

"Why? What kind of person would kill a little kid?" Stoney asked him.

Matt said nothing.

Light had finally begun to filter in the barn from the gray dawn and Stoney could see Matt's face. Matt glared at him. "I guess I better fix you a nice spot to hang from and get on my way."

Matt walked to the door of the barn, opened it a crack, and looked around.

"Stoney, it's gonna be all right," a quiet voice whispered.

Stoney turned his head to the sound and saw nothing. He thought he was dreaming.

He felt the cord being untied and again he heard the voice in his ear. "Stay perfectly quiet, and keep your hands behind you like they are still tied, okay?"

Stoney nodded his head.

He looked around again and saw nothing.

"It's your Uncle Stone. I am gonna help you and your dad get out of here, but you have to do what I say, okay?"

Stoney gulped, "Okay."

Matt turned around and said, "What did you say, kid?"

Stoney sat up straight in his chair.

"Tell him you are talking to your Uncle Stone."

"I was talking to my Uncle Stone."

Matt walked over to stand in front of Stoney looking around. "And where, pray tell, is your Uncle Stone?"

"Heaven," Stoney said without a smile.

Matt threw his head back and laughed. "Well, kid, you're gonna need help from heaven. As a matter of fact, you will probably be there before the morning is over, so I hope he heard you. I guess you will go to heaven, you haven't been a very bad boy have you? I am not so sure about your daddy though."

Stoney glared at him, "I always try to be good, and I know my daddy will go to heaven too, but not you, you creep."

Matt walked over to the door, leaned against the wall, and stared out at the empty countryside. He looked over at Stoney and laughed again.

Bobby heard talking, and he wondered if he was dead because he could distinctly hear Stone Hardaway's voice in his ear.

He opened his eyes and saw Matt Stanley staring out the door. He looked over at Stoney and saw he was okay, and there standing between he and Stoney was Stone. Bobby shook his head and it hurt like crazy. He was pretty sure he was alive, his head hurt too bad to be dead; but there was Stone, smiling that silly smile he used to get when he was real proud of himself.

Stone put his finger over his lip to be quiet and said to Bobby, "Well kid, looks like you got yourself a little predicament here, are you okay?"

Bobby nodded as inconspicuously as possible. When Matt turned around from the door, he closed his eyes again.

Matt looked at Bobby and then at Stoney who was smiling.

Matt glared at Stoney. "What are you smiling at, you little moron?"

Stoney just stared at him and said nothing.

Stone turned around and looked at Stoney and said, "You have to be really cool, Stoney. Don't let on that anything is going on. Can you do that?"

Stoney nodded and frowned. Stone winked at him, "There ya go, you got it."

Stone said, "Here's what we are going to do, Stoney. Now follow me exactly, okay?"

Stoney nodded.

"I am going to take care of this character, but you're gonna have to get over there and get FR out of his stall and ride him out of here. You can ride him to the highway; just follow the tree line and it will take you right to the road. There are a million people out there looking for you."

Stoney whispered, "I'm not allowed to ride him, Uncle Stone. Daddy won't let us ride the big horses."

Matt walked over to Stoney, "Who are you talking to, kid? You can't ride what?"

"I'm talking to my Uncle Stone I told you."

"Well stop it, you're giving me the creeps. You act like he's right here, for Pete's sake."

"He is," Stoney said.

Matt shook his head, "Sheesh, and they say I am crazy."

He went back to the door.

"I am going to yell, *now Stoney*, and when I do, you run over there and open that stall and climb on FR and take off out the door."

"I can't get on him, he's too tall," Stoney said.

"Climb up the stall and slip over on him. You ever ride bareback?"

Stoney nodded, and then he said in a whisper, "But I am not allowed to ride the thoroughbreds. And what about my daddy? I can't leave him here."

Matt glared at him again.

Stone said, "It's okay, I am going to be right behind you, but I want you out of here first. And your Dad has a little debt to settle with this character and then he will be right along with you. Your dad came to save you and he asked me to help, so you just do as I tell you, okay?"

Stoney nodded again. It was so strange to see Uncle Stone. He knew just what he looked like from his pictures, but being able to see him was weird. He felt just like he was dreaming. Stoney knew everything was going to be okay; his daddy was here and he was going to hammer that old Matt Stanley. Stoney just wished he could stay and watch!

Matt looked over at him again and Stoney smiled.

Matt frowned and stuck his tongue out. Stoney returned the gesture.

Bobby felt his hands being untied as he feigned sleep, and Stone whispered to him, "I told Stoney to ride FR out of here, look over at him and let him know it's okay."

Stone turned back to Stoney, "We are going to be all set Stoney, you're going to climb that gate and ride FR out of here, right?"

Stoney looked at Bobby, and Bobby smiled and winked at him. Stoney said, "Okay, Uncle Stone."

Stoney watched Matt at the door and was amazed

to see a board go flying right at Matt's head. It hit him hard and he yelled.

He turned around trying to see where the board came from and then *pow* another crack from the board, this time swung with force. It knocked him to his knees.

Matt was bleeding from a gash in the side of his head. He was trying to get to his feet and holding his head, "I am bleeding. I need something for my head..."

Stoney ran over to the stall, climbed up, and opened the latch. He took FR's bridle and pulled him to the gate so he could climb on. He patted his face and they took off out of the gate and raced from the barn.

"He's all yours, Bobby. I am going to make sure Stoney gets to the road and I will be back for you."

Bobby stood up his head pounding, Matt Stanley was on the barn floor and Bobby wanted to kill him with his bare hands.

He went over, took him by the shirt, and pulled him up to face him. "Now, we can fight fair. You have a headache just like mine."

Matt tried to scream for help but his voice just echoed in the big, empty barn.

Stone walked to the side of the barn and climbed on KingFlint, who had been waiting for him, and rode off after Stoney and FR.

Stoney kept looking back to make sure Matt wasn't following him, afraid that he was just dreaming he had gotten away. FR was happy to be out of the stall and he galloped along seemingly well aware that this wasn't a race and it wasn't a jockey on his back. He was in no rush at all.

Stoney heard hoof beats behind him and when he looked back, he saw KingFlint and Stone.

They galloped along beside him.

"You are a good rider, Stoney. I guess you got that from your dad."

Stoney smiled. "Yes sir. My daddy is the best jockey in the world."

Stone smiled and said, "Yes son, he sure is."

They were finally at the road and there wasn't a car in sight. Stoney pointed up the road and said, "I just live right up there."

"Yes, I know you do. I thought there would be a policeman along here, but I guess you'd better just ride on home. I know some people that are going to be very glad to see you."

"Aren't you coming too, Uncle Stone?"

"I might ride along for a ways, I want to make sure you get there safe and sound. Can you remember how to tell the policemen where to find Matt?"

Stoney nodded. Stoney could see his driveway and his heart raced, "Will you tell my mommy you said for me to ride FR?"

There was no answer. He turned to look back and Stone was gone.

He whistled to FR and they galloped into the driveway and up to the house.

Emma saw them coming before anyone else did.

She pointed and said, " Uh oh, Mommy. Stoney is riding one of the racing horses."

Sandy raced to the door and out to the yard.

"Stoney, Stoney! Oh my gosh, Stoney, are you okay?"

The police and FBI came outside and everyone was talking at once, asking questions, and looking at Stoney to make sure he was all right.

The police had been searching for Bobby, since he seemed to have just vanished into thin air.

Sandy thought she must be dreaming. Here was Stoney riding this high-powered horse bareback, riding up like nothing had happened.

Stoney told the police where they could find Matt and Bobby.

Sandy hugged Stoney so tight he couldn't breathe. He pulled away and said, "Mom, guess what? Daddy came to save me and he asked Uncle Stone to help. Uncle Stone came from heaven and helped me get out of there."

Sandy gasped, "Stoney, is your daddy okay? Where is he?"

Stoney told her what had happened and that Bobby had stayed to give Matt a whipping.

As they stood there talking, Bobby came up the road to the edge of the driveway on the back of King-Flint, holding on to Stone. He slid off and stood there looking at Stone.

"Thanks for saving us, Stone. Thanks for saving my kid."

Stone laughed, "You saved Stoney, kid. He won't

remember anything except that dad came to rescue him. He's a great kid. You and Sandy have done good."

"I know you have to go, but man do I wish you could hang around a while. I really miss you."

Stone smiled at him, "Got that Angel waiting, Bobby. I have to be on my way."

Bobby smiled and said, "Tell her we love her too."

Stone stared at his face and then he pulled the rein and KingFlint turned and they rode out of sight.

Bobby walked up the driveway to his family and the police.

Stoney ran to his daddy and grabbed him around the waist. Then he looked down the drive and said softly, "I guess Uncle Stone went back to heaven."

Agent Sharp looked at Bobby with a question in his eyes and Bobby said, "I will have to explain that one to you later."

Stoney smiled, "Uncle Stone and KingFlint rode with us. We weren't by ourselves. Did you know King-Flint went to heaven, Dad? I didn't know horses went to heaven."

He said to his son, "Well, I think the real good ones go to heaven son, and we know KingFlint was a real good one, don't we?"

Stoney nodded and said, "And so is FR dad, he was real nice to me."

He whispered, "Thank you Lord, thank you for helping my boy."

Stoney sat with the FBI on the porch and told all

that happened. The police and another agent went to the barn and picked up Matt.

Bobby and Don Dowd walked beside FR to the barn and Bobby brushed him, gave him a bucket of oats, and put him in his stall.

"Man, what in the world would make that idiot do something like this?" Don asked. "That little boy could have been killed. I guess you feel better getting to knock some sense into him huh?"

Bobby looked at Don with a serious look. "All I could do was tie him up, I couldn't do anything else because I knew if I started to hit him I wouldn't stop. That was a scary feeling. He's sick. I asked him why he was doing all of this and he said he just wanted to be me.

"He was going to hang Stoney, Bobby said with a catch in his voice. His mother was in a mental institution because she hanged his little brother. She was after him too, but he managed to hide from her. I guess that made him crazy."

Don shook his head. "Wow, that's awful, Bobby. He's gone away for a long time though, probably won't ever get out. Your family is safe now, but what an ordeal."

"Poor Stoney and Emma. This will always be with them."

Don sighed. "Aw, kids are pretty resilient Bobby. They'll be over it in no time."

The police finally left but Agent Sharp stayed and had lunch with the family, trying to reassure them that Matt Stanley wouldn't get out of jail or the mental facility—wherever the courts sent him—for a very long time; if ever.

Don went home to tell Karen about the day's events, and Tom called and said he would be ready to come back to work in a few days.

As Bobby walked Agent Sharp to his car, he glanced up to the sky and saw a rainbow. "Well, would you look at that? Bobby asked. There aren't even any rain clouds left in the sky."

Agent Sharp smiled and said, "It's raining somewhere and you get to enjoy the rainbow. I was always taught that a rainbow was a promise."

Bobby grinned, "Well, I bet I know what this promise is." Agent Sharp waited for him to finish his statement but instead Bobby offered his hand, thanked him for all the work, and said goodbye.

As he pulled out of the driveway, Robert Sharp looked up again at the rainbow and smiled. Today, he felt like a rainbow was exactly what he needed.

. . .

Sandy waited on the porch for Bobby. "I thought when you disappeared that maybe you had been kidnapped too, or worse; maybe decided this was more than you could deal with and just ran away."

Bobby grinned at her. "No you didn't, you wouldn't think that."

She lay her head over on his shoulder, "I couldn't blame you if you did. I felt like I was going to explode."

He took her hand, "Just another lump in the gravy of life."

"Oh my gosh, that was a terrible analogy, and you weren't talking about *my* gravy were you, Mr. Tolliver?" Sandy feigned outrage.

Bobby patted her behind, "Well I don't know, how about you make some gravy and I will see if it fits?"

Sandy stuck out her tongue and ran in the house, calling out to him, "How about *you* make the gravy, and I take a nap?"

Emma and Stoney sat on the couch with the dogs at their feet and smiled at each other as their parents came in the house laughing and talking. Stoney patted his sister's hand, "See, everything *is* okay. After while we will go out to the barn and play with the kittens."

She smiled at her brother with shining eyes, and they skipped off into the kitchen to be near their mom and dad.

EPILOGUE

Angie stood on the bank of a clear, silver lake, her horse grazing just behind her. She smiled as Stone came riding up on KingFlint.

"Well, she said. That didn't take too long."

Stone smiled, "Nope, it went pretty well. You should have seen how brave Stoney was, Angie. That would have scared a grown-up."

"Think they will ever not need you down there?"

Stone laughed, "I think they will be okay. And, I told you I would be back and we could get back to where we were...now, *where* were we?"

Angie smiled at him with twinkling eyes, "You were telling me how you're gonna love me for eternity I think..."

"Hmmmm, Stone said. I thought I was doing this," and he leaned over and kissed her.

"That's right, you *were* doing that, she said. And

I can handle a few more eons of it too if you don't mind, Mr. Hardaway."

"I don't mind a bit, Stone said with a grin. In fact, let's go somewhere so we can really do it right."

"Sounds like heaven," Angie said with a smile. As they climbed on their horses, Stone leaned over and kissed her. They rode up the path and around the hill, out of sight.

GLOSSARY OF TERMS

Track Information and Understanding the Terminology

Horseracing is big business in America and around the world. Thoroughbred horses are bred to run long distances and can run at speeds exceeding forty-five miles per hour. They have very small ankles, not much larger than humans. They are born to run; it is what they love to do.

Quarter horses are bred to run shorter distances and can run at speeds exceeding forty miles per hour. They are generally built stockier than the thoroughbred and are better for pleasure/western riding. The quarter horse has a more even temperament than the high-strung thoroughbred as well.

To watch any horse run is to watch one of God's living works of art.

There are many racetracks across the country, and around the world. Bobby's world is the US, and as a great jockey, he is invited to ride at numerous tracks. I have mentioned just a few of the US tracks in the story. Here is some information about each one.

Racetracks

1. Calder Racecourse in Miami, Florida. A beautiful track owned by the Churchill Downs Corporation. Set in beautiful Miami, with flowers and greenery, and a sandy track is a beautiful backdrop to the sparkling Atlantic Ocean and the sunny Florida sky.

2. GulfStream Park, Hallandale, Florida. Just down the freeway from Calder. Gulfstream was recently remodeled and is now a Racetrack and casino (Racino). Part of the money from the casino helps fund the races, and helps the horsemen and the horses. If you are on the top floor of the track, you can see the ocean just a half mile away. Hallandale is halfway between Miami and Fort Lauderdale, a couple miles from Hollywood, Florida. Gulfstream is home to one of the premier pre-Derby races, the Florida Derby.

3. Aqueduct, New York City; a cavernous monument of horseracing nostalgia. Aqueduct dates back to the late 1800s and can hold a crowd of 60,000 plus. Aqueduct is one of two racetracks in the New York City area. Home to the Wood Memorial one of numerous prestigious stakes races presented annually.

4. Belmont Racetrack, Elmont, New York; another of the NYRA (New York Racing Authority) tracks. Belmont, like Aqueduct, is home to many graded stakes races. Belmont and Aqueduct share the racing calen-

dar, taking turns at racing dates. Some of the greatest horses in history have raced in New York.

5. Saratoga Race Course, Saratoga Springs, New York; upstate New York race track with a short racing schedule. Saratoga is the oldest track in America. It is known as "The Spa" for the wonderful warm springs that run underneath the city. The water is quite drinkable and is very therapeutic. Saratoga is home to the Travers, The Whitney, The Hopeful and so many other prestigious stakes races that trainers all around the country point their horses to a wonderful summer meet at "The Spa." Bring your family and sit among the giant trees and grill a burger, or eat at one of the many little shops featuring food of all types from lemonade to sausage on a stick. You can also join the "beautiful people" in the clubhouse and have a lovely meal in one of the restaurants inside. Saratoga runs the gamut in people watching. Celebrities, athletes; both current and former world greats, the very rich and the not-so-very-rich can be found at Saratoga. The staff encourages the customers to "dress" appropriately. You will see people dressed in everything from hats and dresses from the 1800s to jeans and halter-tops. There is a "beautiful" hat contest several days of the meet; many activities for the kids like face painting and jugglers, and you can relax in the shade and watch the races on one of the hundreds of TVs

hanging in the trees. Truly a family oriented festival of racing in beautiful upstate New York.

6. Lake George: While Lake George is not a racetrack, it is home to the gorgeous lake of the same name, surrounded on three sides by the Adirondack Mountains. Lake George is a beautiful little village that has wonderful shops, quaint hotels and a lot of family related activities such as water parks, boat rentals, and tour boats on Lake George. Situated twenty-five miles north of Saratoga Springs, it is a very relaxing alternative to staying in Albany or in Saratoga Springs on your visit.

7. Arlington Park, Arlington Heights, Illinois, is another racetrack in the Churchill Downs family. Everything about Arlington Park will remind you of summer. From the sparkling white fences to the lush green turf track, flowers of every color and variety and a very up-close and friendly paddock for viewing the horses, Arlington Park dramatizes the "new era" of horseracing. The "theatre" in the simulcast area, large screen televisions on the walls, a plethora of dining options and warm friendly people make Arlington Park a favorite with locals and race fans around the country. Situated west of Chicago, about fifteen miles from O'Hare Airport, you can even ride the train to the entrance of Arlington Park. Home of the very prestigious stakes race, the Arlington Million, as well

as numerous other graded stakes races, Arlington Park is the premier racetrack in the Midwest.

8. Keeneland Race Track, Lexington, Kentucky, is home to the famous Toyota Bluegrass Race among other highly acclaimed three-year-old races. Keeneland is a beautiful track situated across the road from the Lexington Blue Grass Airport. The horses really seem to love Keeneland, they are saddled under the trees where they can relax and nibble on the grass until time to head out on the track. Keeneland is not very far from the Kentucky Horse Park that is home to some great, retired racing champions. Never miss an opportunity to visit this gorgeous place.

9. Downtown Lexington is a few miles from the track, a beautiful drive past some of the most famous horse farms in America. The race meets at Keeneland are short; usually about forty-five days in the spring and thirty-six days during the fall meet. There are a number of nice places to stay in the Lexington area. You will also see lots of famous horse-people while you are there. It is a lovely old track with a lot of class.

10. Churchill Downs, Louisville, Kentucky, is the diamond center in a ring of sparkling jewels. The ultimate racetrack, the one place every racehorse, owner, trainer, jockey, and track maven wants to be. Recently updated and refreshed, the mighty

twin spires stand watch over a gorgeous track and grounds that will take your breath away. Just walking into the grandstands will bring tears to your eyes when you think about the history of the track and the legendary horses and riders who have graced that magnificent track. Of course, the track is owned by the Churchill Downs Corporation and maintained as one would expect of the immortal granddaddy of them all, Churchill Downs. Located not far from the Louisville Airport, Churchill Downs epitomizes the racing industry. The beauty and pageantry of the Kentucky Derby is never far from the minds of every patron. A wonderful museum graces the property and there is a garden where some of the greatest horses in history are buried. Any trip to Kentucky must include a visit to Churchill Downs.

11. Ellis Park, Henderson, Kentucky, was built in 1922 and is home to the Gardenia Stakes every year. Once owned by Churchill Downs, it was almost destroyed by a tornado in 2005. Ellis Park is a beautiful track with a lot of local color, and friendly people. It's smaller grandstand and grounds area makes it very intimate and cozy. It is just down the road from both Keeneland and Churchill Downs and makes a great trifecta of Kentucky tracks to visit. Ron Geary the President/CEO of Ellis Park has committed to making Ellis Park a premier racetrack once again.

12. Fair Ground, New Orleans, Louisiana, is the second oldest track in America. In 2005, Hurricane Katrina tried to destroy the Fair Ground, but she refused to let a little wind and water take her away. Churchill Downs Corporation also owns the Fair Ground purchasing her from a family operation in 2005 shortly before Katrina hit. The people are friendly, and the food is fantastic. It is New Orleans, how can you go wrong? Did you know that some of the greatest jockeys in the United States are Louisiana natives? And many got their first start riding right here at the Fair Ground. Located five miles from the famous French Quarter, the Fair Ground is wrapped around by Gentilly Boulevard. Lots of local color, fun people, and a beautiful track await you. The Fair Ground is the winter track for many horses that normally run in Canada and on the East Coast. Always balmy with tropical temperatures in the low 80s in December, it is a marvelous break for tired horses and weary trainers. When you go, ask for Chef Pat's famous shrimp Po'Boy sandwich. Remember *bon temps roulez*! (Let the good times roll!)

13. Louisiana Downs, Bossier City/Shreveport, Louisiana, is another Racino. Owned by Harrah's for a couple years now, Louisiana Downs is the home of the highly regarded Super Derby, another of the pre-Derby races. The Downs is a classic. There have been many greats run in the Super Derby. Louisiana Downs is one of those tracks that allow you get

up close and personal with the horses and trainers. The fence is the only barrier between the fans and the track and the horses do a post parade almost close enough to touch. There is a lot of fan camaraderie and the horses seem to enjoy this relaxed atmosphere. There are a lot of things to do in the Shreveport/Bossier City area: great fishing, boating, and many good places to eat. There is a Science Place and lots of shopping, or just go relax; there is something for everyone.

14. Lone Star Park, Grand Prairie, Texas, is a Magna Entertainment owned racetrack. Recently celebrating a ten-year reign as the only racetrack in the Dallas-Fort Worth Metroplex, Lone Star Park was host to the 2004 Breeder's Cup. That was quite an honor for a track so "young." The home of the Lone Star Derby and The Texas Million, Lone Star hosts numerous stakes races. They have a summer run from April to late July and then a quarter-horse meet in the late fall. Home to terrific people and a magnificent grandstand featuring murals and paintings by the world famous artist Fred Stone; Lone Star Park is a beautiful example of artistry and design.

15. Santa Anita Park, Arcadia, California, sits at the foot of the San Gabriel Mountains. A ten-minute drive from Pasadena, California; Santa Anita is the beautiful race-place with a rich history of racing. Remember Seabiscuit? He ran there. Many great ones have raced at Santa Anita. Tucked away in

Arcadia, a neat upscale little community, Santa Anita hosts the Santa Anita Derby, another pre-Derby race, as well as scores of other notable stakes races. Be prepared for surprises at the track. You never know when the person standing beside you at the fence is a famous movie star or athlete. Everyone is a racing fan at Santa Anita and it is not at all unusual to be rubbing elbows with the red carpet set. Early morning head over to Clocker's Corner for a delicious breakfast. You will also have a chance to watch famous horses working out on the track and their famous trainers having coffee and staring bleary-eyed at their stopwatches. There is the Seabiscuit Tram tour of the barns and stable area. During live racing, there is a fun infield with lots of activities for the kids. Santa Anita is a grand old track with fun people and great horses.

16. Hollywood Park, Inglewood, California. Across town from Santa Anita, sits the other Southern California racing queen, Hollywood Park. Also once owned by the Churchill Downs Corporation, Hollywood Park boasts some of the best racing in California. A short 5 miles from Los Angeles International Airport, Hollywood Park is near everything. Five miles from the famous Santa Monica Pier, Redondo Beach, the Getty Museum, Beverly Hills, Rodeo Drive and downtown LA. You have the mountains in the distance, the ocean behind

you and beautiful horses on the track. What more could you ask for?

17. Del Mar Race Course, Del Mar, California; where the turf meets the surf. Nothing more inviting than a day at Del Mar during their short summer meet. You can literally look out the end of the grandstand window and see the Pacific Ocean. The horses thrive here in the summer, runs on the beach help strengthen their legs. This place called Del Mar was once the hangout (and the brainstorm) of old-time greats Jimmy Durante, Bing Crosby, and Bob Hope. As a matter of fact, the street that runs in front of the track is called Jimmy Durante Boulevard. There are so many things to do here and you are just 25 miles north of San Diego. Del Mar home of perfect weather, beautiful people, and great racing days like the Pacific Classic. Everything about Del Mar will make you want to return the following summer.

Some other tracks to visit

- Philadelphia Park, Philadelphia PA, a Racino.
- Hawthorne Racetrack, Palatine, IL, just outside Chicago. Home of winter racing and lovely new facilities.
- Monmouth Park, Oceanport, NJ, home of the 2007 Breeder's Cup. Racing at the New Jersey shore.
- Remington Park, Oklahoma City, OK-A very nice new Racino.
- Sunland Park, El Paso, TX-owned by Win Star Casino and home to the Win Star Derby.
- Delta Downs, Vinton, LA-Newly remodeled Racino owned by Boyd Entertainment.
- Evangeline Downs, Lafayette/Oppolousas, LA. A Fun Racino.
- The Fairground, Delta Downs and Evangeline All the best South Louisiana has to offer.
- There are many more tracks, but space won't allow us to list them all. My apologies to any of you that I had to leave off. I will not leave you out of the next list!

Race Track Terminology

1. Jockey: Rider of a racing horse.

2. Trainer: A person who trains horses for themselves and/or others to race. A trainer can have horses running at many tracks, they hire assistants who work with the horses and are usually in daily contact with the trainers.

3. The Paddock: that is the saddling area where the horses are brought from the barn. Usually only the trainer, owners, and the horses' regular handler will be in the paddock.

4. The Gate: A portable/moveable apparatus (usually attached to a tractor) that has twelve gates. These gates are small, only wide enough for a horse to stand in, it has a back gate that shuts as soon as the horse is in; and the front gate is magnetic, opening as soon as the starter pushes the button. It can be pushed open by a horse if they try. Sometimes you will see a horse break through the gate and take off running. The gate didn't malfunction, the horse pressed against it and it opened. This helps cut down on injuries.

5. Outrider: Modern-day cowboys and cowgirls who ride their own horse and watch out for the jockeys and horses in a race. The outriders will sit just a few feet behind the gate or alongside the gate and will follow along as the horses run their race.

On those occasions when a horse loses his jockey (throws him off, or he falls off) the outrider's job is to catch the loose horse before he can create problems for the other horses and jockeys during the race. A horse's natural tendency is to run with the herd so they instinctively head for the other horses. A loose horse can cause injuries for themselves, the jockeys, and the other horses. Outriders are everyone's heroes. They normally ride quarter horses that can accelerate quickly and are not easily intimidated by an anxious animal. It is quite a thrill to watch an Outrider and his horse gain on a loose racehorse, carefully grab his reins and lead him safely back to his trainer.

6. Lead-Pony: As the horses leave the paddock, a rider on another horse takes the reins and leads the horse out to the track. The lead pony stays with the horse past the post parade and until the horse takes off around the track to warm up. They take the reins again when the jockeys bring them back to start loading in the gate. The lead pony hands the reins to a member of the gate crew and then he stays with the horse and jockey until they leave gate.

7. A Meet: Term used for the racing days of a track.

8. Stewards: The officials at every track who look at each race and make sure there was not interference or anything out of the ordinary in the race that

might have caused one horse to lose his chance of bettering his position in the race. Whenever there is a fall, or a jockey objects because he/she thinks another jockey/horse cut in front of him etc. the stewards view the replay of the race from various angles and determine if the horse was at fault or if it was just in the normal flow of the race. The stewards are the final authority of a race. They decide when a race is official. There are usually two to three stewards at each track on a race day.

9. Silks: The silk shirts and pants worn by a jockey during a race. Owners have their own colors and insignia that they use in the design of the jockey's shirts and hat. Many Jockeys have begun wearing Kevlar vests under their shirts. The vests weigh very little and they help protect their ribs in case of a fall.

Race Types

1. Claiming: Claiming races are by far the most common races at every track. A claiming race is basically a race where every horse in the race can be purchased (claimed) for the claiming price of the race. (I.e. $5000 claimers up to $100,000 claimers.) If a trainer wishes to buy (claim) a horse from a particular race, he must put up the money with the Racing Secretary before the race and put his name in the claim box. If there is more than one person wish-

ing to claim a certain horse, then there is a drawing at the end of the race and that person whose name is drawn gets the horse. If the horse wins the race, the current connections get the purse, but the claiming connections get the horse. There are Maiden Claimers and also Claiming Races which have conditions such as Non-Winners of 1,2,or 3 races. Horses in this class must pass through their conditions before they can advance to the higher-class races such as an Allowance Race.

2. Maiden Special Weight: These are non-winning horses whose trainers/owners do not want to sell. Maiden Specials Weights are generally better class horses than the low-level claimers.

3. Allowance: These are races that feature good quality horses racing for substantial purses (cash amounts).

4. Stakes: Stakes races also come in a wide range of dollar values. There are Graded Stakes races that will give the winner, place, and show horses black type in their resume. This is good for breeding purposes. The classier the stakes race; from Grade 1, Grade 2, Grade 3, the more money an owner can charge for breeding. There are Handicap Races that have conditions that a horse must meet before they can run. The best races, the races every horse owner hopes to have a horse for, are the graded stakes races. Good examples of the best of the best races

are the Triple Crown races; The Kentucky Derby, the Preakness and the Belmont; all are Grade 1 races with purses ranging from $750,000 to well over a million. Grades 2 and 3 usually have purses around $250,000 to $150,000, which is divided among the top five finishers in the race. But only the top three finishers get black type from the race.

Distances

1. Furlong: A common measurement of races. Most races are 6 furlongs. Races for younger horses can range from 2 furlongs to 5.5 furlongs. A furlong is one eighth of a mile, 220 yards, 660 feet.

2. Races ranges from short distances like six, seven furlongs, which are called sprints, to distances from 1 mile up to a mile and a half, which are called routes. A horse's breeding determines what their best distance to run will be. More and more horses are being bred for the shorter distances from 5.5 furlongs up to a longer distance of a mile and an eighth. We see fewer and fewer thoroughbred horses being bred for marathon length routes of a mile and a half or longer.